Hidden Treasures
Kathryn Springer

Steeple Hill®

Published by Steeple Hill Books™

STEEPLE HILL BOOKS

Steeple
Hill®

ISBN-13: 978-0-373-87493-4
ISBN-10:   0-373-87493-6

HIDDEN TREASURES

Copyright © 2008 by Kathryn Springer

www.SteepleHill.com

Printed in U.S.A.

In this way they will lay up treasure for themselves as a firm foundation for the coming age, so that they may take hold of the life that is truly life.
—*1 Timothy* 6:19

To Norah—
Always listen for the sound of wild geese,
stop to pick dandelions, study the clouds…
and reach for the stars. And remember,
you are fearfully and wonderfully made!

Prologue

"I knew I'd find you hiding in here."

"Technically, it's not hiding if the person is in plain sight." Meghan McBride shot a mischievous smile at her sister, Caitlin, who sauntered into the room with her usual catlike grace, still wearing the periwinkle-blue stilettos she'd stepped into at eight o'clock that morning.

Meghan had kicked off an identical pair hours ago. It was too much to hope Caitlin hadn't spotted her bare toes peeking out from under the netting of the tea-length gown she wore. She'd probably already noticed that Meghan's hair had managed to break free of the grid of bobby pins anchoring it in place. It wasn't fair that the breeze skipping off Lake Superior during their youngest sister's outdoor wedding ceremony had ignored Caitlin's neat French twist and set its sights on Meghan's mop of curls—the ones the stylist had spent an extra half hour trying to restrain.

"Evie and Sam are getting ready to leave. She was wondering where you were…" Caitlin frowned. "Is that *frosting* on your elbow?"

Shoot. Meghan inspected her arm and made a halfhearted attempt to scrub off the pink smear with her thumbnail. "I think so. I warned Evie that she shouldn't have asked me to cut the cake."

Like a magician, Caitlin somehow produced a delicately embroidered handkerchief out of thin air and handed it to her with a sigh.

That was the trouble with sisters. They knew every chink in a person's armor. Caitlin's sharp eye for detail made her wildly popular as an image consultant and wildly annoying as an older sister. Evie had waved the white flag of surrender and turned her closet over to Caitlin years ago, but Meghan had refused to go down without a fight. She *liked* going barefoot and wearing blue jeans and T-shirts. Not only did she spend most of her spare time with children and paint, every time she bought something new, she ended up getting a stain—or two—on it. What was the point?

"I still can't believe our baby sister is married," Caitlin murmured.

Meghan couldn't believe it, either. The previous summer, she and Caitlin had sweet-talked Evie into managing Beach Glass, their father's antique store, while he went away on a two-week fishing trip. Evie's brief stay had turned into something straight from the pages of an action-adventure novel. She'd discovered that her father and his friend, Jacob Cutter, were searching for clues they hoped would lead them to a sunken ship. Their cautious sister, who ordinarily steered clear of anything risky, had dodged a corrupt group of treasure hunters and fallen in love with Jacob's son, Sam.

"Right out of a fairy tale," Meghan murmured. "Who would have guessed?"

Caitlin made a noise that sounded suspiciously like a snort.

Except that image consultants *didn't* snort. "Sam's a good guy."

The understatement of the year. "He's perfect for Evie. And she deserves to be happy." Meghan knew her sister couldn't argue with that.

"She does." Caitlin's expression softened. "We better get back to the reception before she hunts us down—"

"Too late!" The words, accompanied by Evie's lilting laugh and the rustle of satin, preceded her into the kitchen.

Meghan took one look at her sister and the lump that had lodged in her throat—the one that had formed while she'd watched Sam and Evie recite their vows—swelled to the size of an orange again. Evie looked spectacular in the ivory gown Caitlin had found in an exclusive shop in the Twin Cities, where Caitlin and Meghan lived.

Meghan ignored a pinch of envy. It's not that she wasn't ecstatic for Evie. She just couldn't help but wonder what it would be like to feel that way about someone. Caitlin was openly cynical when it came to love, but Meghan knew it happened to some people. Like their parents. And now Evie and Sam. But for reasons she kept to herself, she wasn't convinced she was ever going to be one of them.

"Sam and I are going to sneak away while the orchestra is playing the last song." Evie's gown swished around her feet as she crossed the room and drew them into an affectionate hug. "I wish I could take you to Paris."

"Oh, Sam would love that," Caitlin said dryly.

"Have fun," Meghan commanded. "And don't worry about Dad. I'm planning to stay until next weekend and I promise I'll take good care of him."

Evie's smile faded slightly, proving she still had some progress to make when it came to letting their father manage on his own. Evie had an exasperating tendency to fuss over Patrick, although Meghan thought she understood why. Evie had been a freshman in high school and the only one of them still living at home when their mother, Laura, had passed away unexpectedly.

"I have a list of reminders—"

Meghan's howl drowned Evie out. "I don't do lists! I lose lists, Evie. You *know* that."

"That's why I made copies." Evie looked smug. "Several of them. And they're posted where you can't miss seeing them."

"On a package of Oreos?" Caitlin said under her breath.

Meghan bit back a protest long enough to glare at Caitlin. When she turned back to Evie, she pasted a smile on her face. No need to upset the bride on her wedding day. "Dad and I will be fine, Evie. Don't worry about a thing."

"Megs is right. It's not like Dad is a toddler who's going to get into trouble the minute your back is turned."

Evie didn't look convinced. "I wouldn't be too sure about that," she said darkly. "Remember what happened last summer."

"The entire Cutter family became believers. Sophie and Jacob got engaged. And you met Sam." Meghan believed in looking at the positives. If she didn't, she'd never have been able to gather the courage to launch her own photography business.

"That's true." Evie gnawed on her lower lip. "But he's up to something. I can always tell. He and Jacob were in a huddle earlier this afternoon and he's been spending a lot of time online lately."

Caitlin opened her mouth but Meghan shot her a warning look and looped an arm around Evie's slim shoulders. "I'll watch out for Dad. And I've got one word for you. *Honeymoon.* Now go. Sam's probably waiting in the car."

Evie's cheeks turned as pink as the miniature roses in her bouquet. "I'm going. And I'll call—"

"When you get back," Caitlin interrupted.

"When I get back," Evie promised.

Meghan didn't believe it for a second. Judging from the skeptical look on Caitlin's face, she didn't, either.

"Evie?" Sam poked his head in the doorway and his pewter gaze zeroed in on his wife. "Are you ready?"

"Just hugging my sisters before we leave."

"There's always time for that." Sam's warm smile encompassed all three women and once again Meghan found herself thanking God that He'd brought Sam and Evie together.

You wouldn't happen to have another Sam hidden somewhere, would you, Lord?

Caitlin cleared her throat. "Go on, you two. The sooner you get out of here, the sooner I get my postcard of the Eiffel Tower."

"I taped a backup list to Caitlin's mirror in case you lose yours," Evie called over her shoulder.

Evie and Sam disappeared and Meghan felt the weight of the sudden silence, knowing that no matter how happy they were for Evie, things would be different now.

"I wish I could stay with you and Dad a few extra days, but I'm booked from now until September." Caitlin broke the silence.

"Dad and I will be fine," Meghan said. "You know Evie. She has a tendency to worry, that's all. Like you said, what kind of trouble can a retired English teacher get into?"

Chapter One

Dad, you are in so much trouble.

Meghan surveyed the papers fanned out on her father's desk. The ones she'd discovered when she'd shouldered her way into the study to deliver his afternoon cup of green tea and plate of Oreos. Evie's list had specified fig bars—in capital letters, no less—but over the course of the week Meghan had fed those to an adorable family of gray squirrels. That the discovery the squirrels liked fig bars had taken place *after* she'd dumped the cookies out the window was entirely coincidental.

She picked up a stack of photos, every one of them depicting a work by a well-known artist named Joseph Ferris. Either her dad had shifted his interest from antiques to art or else he was planning to become an art *thief*.

Which could also explain the blueprints of what looked to be a sizable estate fanned out on the desk blotter.

She'd gotten suspicious when she'd seen the light glowing under the door of her father's study two nights in a row. At midnight. Patrick always went to bed promptly after the ten o'clock news. Both times she'd ignored it, not wanting to draw attention to her late-night forays into the kitchen for leftover wedding cake.

But the night before she'd heard the phone ring a few minutes after twelve and then her father's muffled voice on the other side of the door as she padded down the hallway. She'd assumed he was talking to Evie, but when she'd asked about it at breakfast, her father had almost choked on his whole-grain bagel and mumbled something vague about talking to a friend.

Right. Suspicious, she'd pushed a special code on the phone and listened to a nice little robotic voice recite the number of the last incoming call. From an area code somewhere in upstate New York.

Meghan had to face the truth. Evie's list had turned her into…Evie. But there was no going back now. She had to find out what he was up to.

Ever since Patrick had discovered the whereabouts of the *Noble,* a ship Lake Superior had claimed in the late 1800s, and solved the mystery behind a century-old scandal that had plagued Sophie's family, random people had started to contact him. Some asked for help researching their genealogy while others wanted to hire him to locate missing family heirlooms.

In spite of his daughters' initial misgivings, Patrick had actually taken on some "clients" over the winter and, judging from the growing number of inquiries, his reputation must have spread.

Meghan blew out a sigh. She didn't want to be the wet blanket that snuffed out the fire of enthusiasm in her dad's new hobby, but a person couldn't be too careful nowadays. Hadn't Patrick learned that lesson the summer before, when a man he'd thought he could trust had turned on him and Jacob Cutter while they'd searched for the *Noble?*

She put down a photo of Joseph Ferris's haunting water-color *Momentum* and pivoted toward the door. And came nose to nose with her father.

"*Meghan.*"

"Dad." Meghan crossed her arms and did her best imita-tion of Caitlin. It must have worked, because a deep red stain crept out from under the collar of her father's oxford shirt and worked its way to his cheekbones.

Patrick coughed. "Ah…I was wondering where you were."

I'll bet you were.

"It's three o'clock. Tea and cookie time."

"My watch must be slow," Patrick muttered.

Meghan sighed and decided to stop being Evie. And Caitlin. Especially Caitlin. Her suspicions were ridiculous. This was her father. Patrick McBride. The absentminded professor. Mr. Integrity himself.

"Why the sudden interest in Joseph Ferris, Dad? And please tell me that you aren't planning to supplement your retirement income by becoming an art thief." Meghan laughed.

Patrick didn't. Instead he gave her a thoughtful look. "Do you think it falls under the label of *stealing* if a person is taking something back that technically belonged to them in the first place?"

Meghan groped for the plate of Oreos she'd set on the desk. "Does the something that *technically* belongs to someone else happen to be a work by Ferris?"

"Yes."

Meghan shoved a cookie in her mouth. Never mind twist-ing the two sides apart and delicately scraping out the cream center. "You're going to…to *steal* a Joseph Ferris?"

Patrick smiled. "Of course not. I wouldn't begin to know what an authentic Ferris even looks like."

"Well, that's a relief—"

"That's why I was hoping you'd do it."

"Let me get this straight." An hour later Meghan had a new appreciation for Evie's suspicions about their dad's dedication to his side business. Her younger sister had tried to warn her, after all. "A woman named Nina Bonnefield contacted you by e-mail, claiming she knew Ferris personally. He supposedly left a gift for her on an estate he visited in northern Wisconsin almost *twenty years* ago. And she hired you to find it for her."

"That's it in a nutshell," Patrick said, way too cheerfully in Meghan's opinion.

Of their own volition, Meghan's fingers walked across the desk toward the plate of Oreos. Until she realized she'd eaten them all. "Why doesn't this Nina Bonnefield go back to the estate and retrieve it herself? If it really belongs to her."

There, she'd said it.

"That's…complicated."

Of course it was. "Dad, this whole thing sounds kind of fishy to me. You said she isn't even sure if the gift Ferris left for her was a painting. Maybe it was a coffee mug. Or a souvenir toothpick holder."

"For reasons Nina—*Ms. Bonnefield*—can't share, she can't go back. That's why she needs my help. There's a rumor the island is going up for sale and—"

"Wait a second. Did you say *island?*" Meghan interrupted.

"The Halloway estate is on a private island on Blue Key Lake, near the Chequamegon National Forest. It's been in the family for years but they closed it up in the late eighties."

Halloway. Halloway. The name stirred up something in Meghan's subconscious, but another thought darted in and pushed that one aside for the moment.

"So Nina is somehow related to the family that owns the island?"

Patrick's gaze bounced around the room and finally came to rest on Meghan. "No offense, but I promised Ms. Bonnefield I'd keep that part confidential. Jacob and I checked out her story, and both of us believe she's telling the truth. She sent me a copy of the letter from Ferris and it does sound as if he left something for her. A thank you of some sort for her friendship and encouragement."

"That would be some thank-you," Meghan muttered.

"His paintings are valuable?"

"Paintings, drawings, sculptures. He dabbled in everything. Ferris is one of those artists who gained fame post-mortem. By the time the critics finally noticed him and acknowledged his genius, he was in the final stages of pancreatic cancer. The collection of his work isn't all that sizable because his career was short, so what's out there got snapped up right away. If there's still one floating around, I'm sure someone would have noticed. It may have already been sold."

"Or tucked away in a closet on an estate in northern Wisconsin."

And Meghan thought *she* was an optimist.

She tucked her teeth into her bottom lip and tried to figure out a way to discourage her father from getting himself into a potentially sticky situation. And helping oneself to a valuable piece of art definitely fell into that category, no matter who claimed ownership. "There has to be a way Nina Bonnefield can find out if the Ferris is there without involving *you*."

"There is a reason, but I can't tell you what it is. It's—"

"Confidential. I know." She hated to ask the obvious. "So what's your plan?"

Patrick's eyes lit up and Meghan tried not to groan. Somehow she knew she wasn't going to like the answer.

"The house is going to be opened up temporarily for a family wedding in a few weeks. According to my sources—"

Meghan blinked. *His sources?*

"—after the wedding, the Halloways plan to auction off the contents of the house before the actual sale of the island goes through. From what I've heard, the family used to be quite a patron of the arts. There's a sizable collection of paintings and sculptures there. I'm more familiar with antiques, so I wouldn't be much help."

Meghan's eyes narrowed. She had a background in art. She remembered what *her* dad had initially said about *her* finding the Ferris. She'd assumed he'd been kidding. Now she wasn't so sure.

"Dad, please tell me you aren't thinking I'm a shoo-in for the job."

"Of course not, sweetheart." Patrick looked surprised by the suggestion. "I told Ms. Bonnefield you're a photographer."

That much was true. Meghan relaxed a little, relieved she and her dad were on the same page. It didn't sound like either of them would be of much use to the mysterious Ms. Bonnefield. Thank goodness.

"So she decided to find someone else to play Nancy Drew?"

"Not quite." Patrick plucked off his glasses and rubbed them against his shirttail.

Warning bells suddenly went off in Meghan's head. That

particular gesture meant her father was either nervous—or stalling. *"Daaaad?"*

"I had no idea she was going to pull a few strings."

"What *kind* of strings?"

"Parker Halloway has hired you as her wedding photographer."

"Wedding…" Meghan surged to her feet. "I don't photograph *people.* Didn't you tell Ms. Bonnefield that?"

"I did." Patrick smiled. "But she made you an offer I couldn't refuse."

Meghan's teeth rattled in her head as the small fishing boat bounced over the waves toward Blue Key Island. She kept her gaze trained on the slate-shingled roof peeking through a shield of poplar trees. Proof, at least, that one of Nina Bonnefield's claims was true. The Halloway house really did exist.

Meghan sincerely hoped the woman hadn't been making up the rest of the story.

She still couldn't believe she'd adjusted her work schedule to accommodate a visit to the Halloway estate in the first place. But like Joshua scoping out the Promised Land, a reconnaissance mission was all Meghan would agree to. Unlike her father, she didn't trust a woman who'd suddenly appeared out of cyberspace, claiming a friendship with a famous artist but not willing to disclose the nature of her sketchy relationship with the Halloways. Or why she couldn't simply knock on the door and ask for her property back.

It took several days of negotiations with Patrick, but in the end Ms. Bonnefield had reluctantly accepted Meghan's terms. If Meghan happened to spot an authentic Ferris hanging on the wall, it was up to its owner to figure out a way to claim it.

Meghan didn't trust Ms. Bonnefield but she trusted her dad. And it wasn't his fault that the thought of hunting for a work of art wasn't nearly as nerve-racking as playing wedding photographer. Even though she couldn't argue with Patrick's assertion that it made sense for her to be in a position where she could wander around the island—and the house—with a camera.

The boat tripped over a wave and Meghan grabbed the side to steady herself.

"It's a little choppy today," Verne Thatcher shouted above the roar of the outboard motor. "Storm's moving in quicker than they predicted."

Meghan glanced from the grizzled old fishing guide to the batting of dark clouds unfolding across the sky.

She and Patrick had spent the better part of the afternoon roaming through the sleepy little town of Willoughby, trying to find someone with a boat who was willing to take her across. With a major thunderstorm in the forecast, no one seemed eager to go out on the water. Or maybe it had something to do with the reason for Meghan's trip to the island.

Judging from the closed expressions on the faces of the locals whenever Meghan and Patrick mentioned the name *Halloway,* it was clear the family wasn't going to win any popularity contests. Meghan didn't want to speculate as to the reason why.

Close to giving up, they'd settled into a booth at the local diner to discuss their options when a shadow fell across Meghan's laminated menu.

The man standing beside their table was short and wiry, with features that looked as if they'd been carved from a piece of teak. Dressed from head to toe in field khaki, the only thing that prevented him from looking like a game warden was the Hawaiian-print handkerchief casually knotted at his throat.

He flicked the brim of his hat, which was studded with fishing lures. "Hear you're looking for a boat to the island. We better get there before the rain does."

Meghan barely had time to kiss her dad goodbye before Verne Thatcher tossed her suitcase into the back of his rusty pickup and hoisted her into the cab, where she found herself wedged between two damp, liver-spotted spaniels named Smith and Wesson.

Now, close enough to the island to see the dock jutting out from the gentle contours of the shoreline, a fresh crop of doubts stirred up the butterflies in Meghan's stomach. Just as a raindrop splashed against the back of her hand.

"Someone expecting you?" Verne barked the question as he eased back on the throttle and the boat agreeably slowed down.

"Yes."

It was the truth. They just weren't expecting her to arrive a full week before the wedding.

She'd talked to Parker Halloway's wedding planner, a young woman named Bliss Markham, on the phone the day before and told her that she wanted to come a few days early to find the best spots for a photo shoot. Bliss thought it was a marvelous idea. She'd even repeated the word *marvelous* several times. In the same sentence.

Listening to the woman's fake British accent fade in and out, Meghan thought it was a good thing her father had drafted her for the mission instead of Caitlin. Caitlin would have made mincemeat out of Bliss Markham.

According to Bliss, she wouldn't be the only one on the island. The caretaker, a man the wedding planner had simply referred to as "Bert" and who apparently lived on the estate year-round, was also expecting a landscape team hired to spruce up the grounds and a cleaning service to tackle the inside of the house.

Verne muttered something under his breath. "When I pull up to the dock, jump out and grab your stuff."

Meghan blinked. "Why?"

Verne pointed to the sky, where lightning flickered in the underbelly of a dark bank of clouds. "That's why."

Meghan quickly judged the distance between the dock and the house now visible through the trees. Her breath caught in her throat as she got a close look at it for the first time. She'd never believed in love at first sight. Until now.

For some reason she'd expected the Halloway estate to be a typical north-woods vacation home hewn from rustic logs. Instead it looked as if someone had plucked a château out of the French countryside and deposited it on an island in the middle of a chilly Wisconsin lake.

Meghan forgot about the rain as her eyes absorbed the two-story house painted a sleepy blue, with faded poppy-red shutters and a multicolored slate roof.

Smith and Wesson roused from their nap and lifted their noses, sniffing the air. Then looked accusingly at Meghan.

She figured out why a few seconds later when the heavens opened up.

"Mr. Thatcher, you should come with me up to the house until the rain stops," she shouted over the pelting rain.

Verne's eyebrows met over the bridge of his nose. "No, thanks. I'll take my chances on the water," he shouted back.

Before Meghan could respond to the cryptic remark, her

suitcase sailed out of the boat and bounced onto the dock. She had no choice but to follow it. When she turned to thank Verne for his trouble, the boat was already spearing a path through the waves toward the opposite shore.

Meghan lifted the suitcase and held it over her head. The lopsided old boathouse built on stilts over the water wasn't nearly as charming as the château, but it was probably dry.

The light show dancing in the clouds above her head helped make up her mind. Meghan tucked the camera bag under the hem of her shirt and made a break for it.

Fumbling with the rusty latch, she shouldered the door of the boathouse open and tossed her suitcase in first to protect the bag of Oreos she'd stashed inside of it.

Her eyes adjusted to the gloom of the boathouse more quickly than her nose adjusted to the musty smell emanating from a mound of moldy life jackets stacked in the corner.

From the sound of the rain battering the window, Meghan guessed she'd be stuck here awhile. She wrung the water out of her hair, wrestled a sweatshirt out of the bottom of the suitcase and pulled it on over her wet T-shirt. Picking through a mishmash of garden furniture, she unearthed an old wicker rocking chair. Minus the cushion.

Meghan settled into it and tucked the headphones from her iPod into her ears, while she attacked the first row of cookies, vowing to stop after four. Or five.

Closing her eyes, Meghan let the praise music wash over her. If she couldn't work in her studio, music was the next best thing to guide her thoughts back to God. And at the moment, she knew she needed a long conversation with Him so she wouldn't unravel at the seams.

I don't have a clue what you have planned, Lord, but here I am. Or here am I, as Isaiah would say. I'd rather photograph animals than people, but I want to help out Dad. For some reason he thinks Ms. Bonnefield is a wounded soul—and you know Dad can never turn his back on a wounded soul.

Something she and her father had in common.

Meghan's "Amen" came out in a yawn, reminding her she'd been up since dawn. She pushed aside the package of Oreos and decided to rest her eyes for a minute. When the rain subsided, she'd find the caretaker and explain why she'd shown up a week early.

The lightning had moved *inside* the boathouse.

Meghan's eyelashes fluttered and she realized she must have dozed off for a few minutes. Confused, she blinked at the bright beam of light aimed directly at her face. It wasn't lightning. It was a flashlight.

Panic suddenly slammed her heart against her chest.

Because on the other end of the flashlight was a…man. The shadows obscured his features but she could see the broad outline of his shoulders as he loomed above her.

She struggled to sit up, shielding her eyes with one hand. "Are you the caretaker?" She croaked. Rats. What was his name? She couldn't remember. "Mr. Um…"

The light suddenly shifted from her face, trailing a path down her soggy frame and lingering a moment on the package of Oreos balanced on her knee.

"Bert," he finally said.

Meghan wondered if all the men in the area had something against speaking in complete sentences. She plucked the head-phones out of her ears—no wonder she hadn't heard him sneak up on her—and pushed her fingers self-consciously through her tangled curls.

Way to make a first impression, Megs. Soaking wet and sound asleep. And probably smelling a bit more like Smith and Wesson than a person in polite company should smell.

Not that the present company seemed very polite…

She took a deep breath. "It's nice to meet you. I'm Meghan McBride."

"You're the…wedding planner?"

Meghan's laugh rippled around the boathouse. He thought she was Bliss Markham? Caitlin would be on the floor when she heard that one.

"No. I'm the wedding *photographer.*"

Chapter Two

And Cade had assumed the day couldn't possibly get any worse.

Since breakfast, he'd had three phone calls from his aunt Judith, all reminding him about wedding details he'd rather forget. The owner of a local landscaping business had been next, telling him they were backing out of the agreement "for reasons they'd rather not discuss." This meant Aunt Judith had been calling them with reminders, too. But they had the luxury of being able to simply walk away from her constant micromanaging. Unlike Cade, who was family. All he could do was exercise the self-control his father had spent years developing in him and attempt to bring some sanity into the nightmare everyone else insisted on referring to as a wedding.

In the afternoon he'd had a surreal twenty-minute conversation with a woman named Bliss Markham, whose voice fluctuated between a clipped British accent one minute and a Southern drawl the next.

And then he'd lost the dog.

And accidentally found the wedding photographer.

He hadn't even known his sister had hired one. The last he'd heard, Parker had decided against a professional photographer and wanted disposable cameras available for the guests. Cade had a hunch Aunt Judith had had something to do with the latest reversal in plans.

His lips twisted. Aunt Judith had something to do with most of the changes made in the past few weeks. When she hadn't been able to change Parker's mind about her choice of a groom, she'd retaliated by attempting to take over everything else instead.

Not that Cade blamed her. It was a Halloway family trait they all shared to some degree.

A polite cough yanked his attention back to the moment. And to the woman sprawled in the wicker chair.

Staring down at Meghan McBride, Cade pushed aside the unwelcome thought that she looked like a pre-Raphaelite model come to life. Oval face. Wide-spaced, gray-green eyes. Damp copper curls spilling over her shoulders. The only thing that didn't fit was the wide, engaging smile on her face.

Cade suddenly realized she'd extended her hand. Time to play nice. He reached out and closed his fingers around hers, but instead of immediately releasing his grip, he drew her to her feet.

It was getting late and he still had to find the dog.

Something hit the floor and Meghan McBride gave a startled yelp. Cade pointed the flashlight down and watched sandwich cookies roll away in every direction.

Meghan's sigh echoed around the room. "Did you ever have one of those days?"

Cade turned toward the door, surprised by a sudden urge to smile. "Never."

"Right." The undercurrent of laughter in her voice sent Cade off balance. And he wasn't sure he liked the feeling.

There'd been more than enough upheaval in his life over the past few weeks. The only reason he'd returned to the island was to tour the estate before meeting with the Realtor. He hadn't voluntarily signed up for his sister's unexpected waltz down memory lane, but when Parker had gotten wind of his plan to sell Blue Key Island, she'd insisted on getting married there.

At least one of them had fond memories of the place.

"I guess I must have dozed off for a few minutes." Meghan McBride's voice had the kind of lilting cadence that sounded as if she were reciting poetry. It should have been annoying. But it wasn't. It was…soothing.

Cade circled the flashlight on the wall until he spotted the switch, hidden beneath a stained baseball cap on a hook just above it. He'd avoided the boathouse since his arrival, but suddenly a hat brought back a whole lot of memories he didn't have the energy or desire to sort through at the moment. Maybe never.

He flipped the light on and turned his attention back to Meghan. Her lips moved as she silently counted the number of edible cookies left in the package.

"Care to explain why you're in the boathouse?" *And why I didn't have a clue you were arriving today?*

"It started to rain the minute we docked. This was closer than the house."

"Who brought you over?" Cade took a quick inventory of Meghan's belongings—a small suitcase, a duffel bag and a camera case—and wondered where she'd stowed the rest of her things.

"Mr. Thatcher," she murmured distractedly.

"Verne Thatcher?"

The incredulous note in the caretaker's voice made Meghan lose count. She glanced up at him and felt the same jolt of stunned surprise when she'd caught her first glimpse of the house.

The man scowling at her didn't *look* like a caretaker. Or a *Bert*.

When Bliss had mentioned the estate's caretaker, Meghan's imagination had immediately conjured up a middle-aged, scruffy-looking hermit in practical coveralls who puttered around the lonely estate, making sure the pipes didn't freeze in the winter.

So much for her imagination.

This caretaker wasn't middle-aged…or scruffy-looking. Unless a person considered the faint shadow that outlined his angular jaw *scruffy*. And Meghan decided, charitably, not to. Hair as dark and sleek as an otter's pelt lay flat against his head, a testimony to the fact she hadn't been the only one caught in the downpour earlier.

The pristine-white polo shirt and tan cargo pants he wore looked more suitable for an afternoon of sailing than for physical labor, but it was Friday. Maybe he had the weekends off.

"You said *Thatcher* brought you over?"

Meghan had been so distracted by the man's looks she'd forgotten he'd asked her a question. And then their eyes met and she found herself distracted all over again. Given his coloring, his eyes should have been chocolate-brown. Or hazel. Not a startling shade of dark blue that reminded her of a summer sky right after sunset.

He arched a brow and Meghan's face heated. "We met Mr. Thatcher at the café in Willoughby," she said quickly.

"We?"

"My dad and I." Meghan watched the cobalt eyes narrow and guessed the reason. He probably thought his peaceful island had come under siege. "We didn't know where to leave my car, so Dad dropped me off until after the wedding."

"Is the wedding ever going to be over?" he muttered, plowing his fingers through his hair as he stalked toward the door. Meghan assumed it was a hypothetical question. "You can go up to the house until I figure out where to put you. There's a fire in the library."

"What are you going to do?"

He threw an impatient look over his shoulder. "I lost… something. And I have to find it before it gets any later."

Meghan scrambled to collect her belongings and managed to squeeze through the door just before it closed. She hurried to catch up with him. "I'll help you."

There wasn't a hitch in his long-legged stride. "Not necessary, Miss McBride."

"Two are better than one, for they have a good return for their work." It was a verse from Ecclesiastes Meghan liked to use to encourage Caitlin when she went into control-freak mode. He shot Meghan a look that should have sent her scurrying for cover. If she was the scurrying kind. Which she wasn't.

"We're…*I'm*…looking for a dog. A spoiled-rotten, annoying, undisciplined dog."

Meghan would have laughed except it looked as if he meant every word. "Does this, um, spoiled, annoying, undisciplined dog have a name?"

"Of course it has a name," he replied irritably.

Someone had definitely skipped the Mister Rogers' episode about good manners. "Dogs *have* been known to respond when their owner calls their name."

"That might work. *If* I were the ungrateful rodent's owner."

The animal lover in Meghan rose up in immediate protest. Points for good looks, major demerits for the rodent comment.

"What kind of dog is it?" Meghan followed him onto a footpath that disappeared into the woods. Only the flashlight beam Bert swept back and forth kept her from tripping over the roots that had erupted through the hard-packed soil.

"I told you."

"You told me it was annoying and spoiled—"

"And undisciplined."

"Right." Meghan cleared her throat. "That may or may not describe its temperament. But what *breed* of dog is it?"

"Some kind of powder-puff thing." The words came out grudgingly.

"I don't think the American Kennel Club officially registers those." Meghan heard a snort from the shadow moving ahead of her.

She stumbled over another root and dropped the duffel bag she now wished she'd left at the boathouse. Pressing a hand to the stitch in her side, she made an executive decision. She put her fingers between her lips and let loose a piercing whistle.

The flashlight beam pooled on the path and then swung in her direction. "If you wanted to get my attention, all you had to do was tap me on the shoulder."

Meghan planted her hands on her hips. "Actually, I'm trying to get the *dog's* attention. But it would help if I knew his name."

Silence.

"This is crazy, Mr...." Was Bert his first or last name? She had no idea. "He could be two feet away—" *Hiding from you.*

"But if the storm scared him, he won't come out unless he hears a familiar voice call his name."

"It's a she," he finally said. "Miss Molly. And please don't sing the words to the song," he added swiftly. "It's been done before. Frequently."

Meghan hummed a bar instead and heard Bert groan. She grinned, not sure why she took such delight in irritating him. She didn't even know the man. "Thank you. Now we're getting somewhere. *Miss Molly—*"

Her lips had barely gotten the words out when a small, furry object suddenly hurtled out of the brush and bumped against her leg, whimpering. Meghan lifted Miss Molly up and cuddled the animal against her chest. From the shape of the dog and its soft coat, she guessed it was a bichon. "I think I found her."

He turned around and strode back down the path, eyeing the bedraggled animal in disgust when he reached Meghan's side. "It's about time."

You're welcome, Meghan thought. If he would have swallowed his manly pride and simply called the dog by her name, they probably wouldn't have had to trek through the woods to find her.

Miss Molly wiggled in Meghan's arms and gazed adoringly at Bert.

Hey, who was the one who rescued you? Meghan wanted to remind her. *This guy called you a rodent....*

Bert stripped off his lightweight nylon jacket and tucked it around the dog. Then he took Meghan's duffel bag and slung it over his shoulder. "Let's go."

Meghan smiled as she followed him back down the trail. So there *was* a heart beating underneath the little polo player embroidered on his shirt.

When they emerged from the woods, Bert ignored the flagstone path and cut across the yard toward the house. Meghan could see a collection of strange silhouettes in the shadows and silently kicked herself for falling asleep in the boathouse. Now she'd have to wait until morning to explore the island.

"Did you find her?" Light spilled onto the grass as a woman suddenly appeared in the doorway.

"We found her," Bert replied tersely.

"We?"

Meghan felt a sudden urge to jump behind a shrub as the woman's head turned in her direction. For the hundredth time that day she wondered what she'd gotten herself into. Or, more accurately, what had her dad and Nina Bonnefield gotten her into? And why had she agreed?

Because Ms. Bonnefield had somehow figured out that while Meghan wouldn't be swayed by a generous personal check, the offer of a sizable donation to a ministry close to her heart would tip the balance in her favor.

"Come inside, both of you. You must be soaked to the skin." The woman stepped back as they reached the semicircle of flagstones in front of the weathered red door. The elements had stripped most of the original paint away and left the lion's head door knocker tarnished.

What exactly was the caretaker taking care of? That's what Meghan wanted to know.

She unveiled Miss Molly and the little dog almost leaped out of her arms when she spotted the other woman standing in the hall.

Their reunion gave Meghan a chance to covertly study Miss Molly's owner. She looked to be in her late fifties, but the combination of a petite figure and ash-blonde hair, shot with silver and cut in a short, low-maintenance style, gave her an almost pixielike appearance.

"I take it she belongs to you." Meghan gently eased the dog into the woman's arms but not before Miss Molly swiped Meghan's cheek in a polite doggy thank-you.

"She does, but over the past few days, I think she's decided she'd rather belong to *him*." The woman's eyes sparkled behind delicate gold-framed glasses. "That's how she got lost. She snuck out of the house and went looking for her new friend."

Meghan hid a smile when Bert winced.

"Follow me. I have a fire going in the library. I know it's the middle of summer but on nights like this, there's nothing more comforting than a cup of tea in front of the fireplace."

Meghan liked the woman immediately.

"I'm Meghan McBride. The wedding photographer." Maybe if she said it often enough, it would eventually sink in.

"Elizabeth Ward. But call me Bert—everyone does."

"Bert?" Meghan frowned.

"I'm the caretaker here."

"But he told me that *he* was the caretaker." Confused, Meghan shot a glance at the man who'd dropped into the chair closest to the fire and stretched out his long legs.

The woman frowned and shook her head. "Cade, what on earth are you up to?"

Meghan glowered at him. *Yes, Cade, what are you up to?*

"I didn't tell you I was the caretaker," he said mildly. "You couldn't remember the name, so I simply told you what it was. Filled in the blank, so to speak."

Meghan silently replayed their conversation and realized he was right. Drat the man. But he must have known she'd assume he was Bert and he hadn't bothered to correct her. "Then who are you?"

"Cade Halloway."

"Cade *Halloway*," she repeated. "But that means—"

The sudden glint in his eyes did nothing to calm the sudden surge in her heart rate as he finished the sentence she couldn't.

"I'm your boss."

Meghan stared up at the ceiling, wrapped in a cocoon of butter-soft blankets, and wondered if she could swim to shore before anyone noticed she was missing.

Cade Halloway's unexpected presence on the island was a glitch she hadn't been prepared for.

A very attractive glitch.

Meghan ruthlessly pushed the thought aside. Maybe he was attractive but he seemed way too serious and uptight. And he had the same keen, watchful look in his eyes that Caitlin had. The kind that said nothing got past him.

It would make her reconnaissance mission that much harder.

Meghan knew there'd be family members arriving for the wedding, but she'd hoped to have enough time to wander freely around the house and grounds without raising anyone's suspicions. On the day of the wedding, she'd smile, snap some photos, convince her father there was no Ferris on the premises and go home.

Meghan shifted restlessly and lavender stirred the air. She inhaled deeply and burrowed into the feather mattress. The upstairs room she'd been assigned to, a cozy nook tucked under the slanted eaves, was perfect. Thanks to Bert. There'd been a few uncomfortable moments in the library when Cade

Halloway had suggested Meghan spend the night in one of the small cabins located on the other side of the island. Bert insisted on putting her up in the main house.

"The cleaning service hasn't shown up yet and those cabins are first on the list. They haven't been aired out in years. Meghan wouldn't sleep a wink."

"Oh, I don't think Miss McBride has trouble falling asleep," Cade had murmured.

The memory of Cade catching her napping in the boat-house instantly surfaced. But even though Meghan now knew who he was, she refused to be intimidated. So she'd smiled sweetly and agreed with him.

"I'm sure they're full of mice." Bert, bless her heart, had tried again.

Cade had shrugged. "Miss McBride seems to like rodents."

Meghan had choked back a protest while Bert folded her arms across her bright red Wisconsin Badgers sweatshirt. "Cade, there are plenty of empty rooms in the house. You can't possibly—"

"Please, I don't want to be a bother." Meghan saw the light of battle in Bert's eyes and jumped into the fray. Even though Bert seemed to be comfortable enough with Cade Halloway to call him by his first name, she didn't want to get the woman into trouble with her employer. "You weren't expecting me to show up this early. I can sleep right here on the sofa…."

"That's not necessary." Cade had abruptly risen to his feet, his expression remote. "Bert will get you settled and in the morning, you can tell me about yourself. And how Parker found you."

Meghan plopped a pillow over her head, stifling a groan. No wonder she couldn't sleep.

She couldn't tell Cade Halloway either of those things.

Chapter Three

Cade woke up to the haunting, liquid cry of a loon on the lake.

Forty-eight hours ago, his alarm clock had been the low keen of sirens and the rhythmic pulse of rush-hour traffic outside the window of his condo in St. Paul.

He glanced at his watch and closed his eyes. Ordinarily he'd be showered, dressed and pulling into the Starbucks' drive-thru by now. Not still horizontal in the twin bed he'd slept in as a child. Even the comforter was familiar—a lumpy bundle of goose down sandwiched between two soft pieces of flannel.

Cade's nose twitched. The blanket even *smelled* the same. A pleasing blend of sunshine and cedar that whisked him back in time. Whether he wanted to go there or not.

In fact, it seemed as if the entire estate had been frozen in some sort of time capsule. Nothing had been updated. Or repaired. Even though Cade knew no one in his family had set foot on Blue Key in years, he'd still been shocked at how neglected the house looked when he'd arrived. The paint on the shutters had bubbled and faded. Scabs of dark moss crusted the roof. The flower gardens his mother had lovingly tended during their summer visits had turned into a matted tangle of weeds.

Douglas Halloway, Cade's father, had refused to sink a penny into the place for twenty years. Except for the generous weekly paychecks mailed to Bert.

Bert.

Cade winced and closed his eyes. He hadn't seen her for years—had to admit he'd all but forgotten his mother's best friend—but from the moment he'd stepped onto the dock, she'd fussed over him as if he were ten years old again. It didn't seem to matter that his presence on Blue Key Island meant she was about to lose both her job and her home.

Cade reminded himself that Bert had to have known the estate would eventually be sold. And she'd been well-compensated over the years for simply *living* in the house. But knowing those things still didn't prevent him from feeling like a first-class jerk.

Especially when Bert treated him with the same indulgent affection and warmth she had when he was a boy, scratched and dirty from climbing the birch tree on the point or dripping water on the floor as he raided the refrigerator for an afternoon snack.1

He hadn't given Bert more than a few hours' notice about his arrival…or Parker's upcoming wedding…and yet she'd hugged him fiercely when he'd arrived and told him that he had his mother's eyes.

Cade was glad his father hadn't been there to hear Bert's observation. He'd spent years making sure his children didn't resemble Genevieve in any way. But not even Douglas Halloway, as powerful as he was, could change the color of a person's eyes.

The sun shifted a fraction of an inch, recreating a stencil of the lace curtain on the scuffed hardwood floor. For the first time Cade noticed a water stain in the corner of the ceiling above the window and mentally adjusted the price of the house. Again.

Whoever bought the island would probably raze the place and put up a structure more suited to its surroundings. He hadn't listed the island with a Realtor yet, but already he'd had inquiries from a developer interested in building a luxury lodge catering to executives-turned-weekend-anglers.

Guys like him.

Not that it mattered what happened to the place after it sold, Cade reminded himself. He had a job to do and the sooner he wrapped things up, the sooner he could get back to civilization. And his business. It had taken a long time for Douglas to turn over the reins to the family's architectural firm and Cade didn't want his father to regret the decision.

Murmured voices, followed by a ripple of delighted laughter, drifted under the door. And worked its way right under his skin.

Meghan McBride. Memories of the evening before came rushing back to Cade and guilt sawed briefly against his conscience. He hadn't exactly been a model host. Okay, he'd been downright rude. He wasn't sure why he hadn't told her who he was when they'd met in the boathouse. Maybe he could put it down to a day that had, thanks to Aunt Judith and a bichon frise that wouldn't let him out of her sight, spiraled out of control. And Cade didn't like it when things got out of control.

Or when something disrupted his concentration. And at the moment, his concentration centered on getting the estate ready to sell. He didn't have time to play the attentive host. Not even to the wedding photographer. Maybe *especially* to the wedding photographer, whose winsome smile just might make him forget he hadn't come to Blue Key to relax and enjoy the scenery.

After he interviewed Meghan and discovered why she'd shown up a full week before the wedding, he'd settle in behind the old oak secretary in the library and start making a list of the contents of the house. And try to hire a new landscaper.

The unmistakable smell of bacon and maple syrup teased his senses and Cade pushed himself out of bed, resigning himself to renewing his gym membership when he got back to the Cities. He'd forgotten how much Bert loved to cook. The day before she'd caught a stringer of bluegills off the dock and fried them up for supper in a cast-iron skillet the size of a hubcap.

He'd told Bert he didn't expect her to cook for him, but she wouldn't listen. In fact, she'd informed him in no uncertain terms that she got tired of cooking for one and he should just "simmer down" and let her spoil someone besides Miss Molly for a change.

And judging from the feminine laughter coming from the kitchen, it sounded as though Bert had added another person to her list of people to spoil.

Good. If Bert kept Meghan McBride company, he wouldn't have to.

Fifteen minutes later Cade padded into the kitchen. Meghan stood guard at the stove, tending Bert's favorite skillet. Barefoot and wearing loose-fitting jeans with a white shirt knotted at her waist, she didn't look old enough to be an established businesswoman.

But her unconventional clothing wasn't what made Cade's breath hitch in his throat. The night before she'd looked as wet and bedraggled as Miss Molly. But the hair he'd assumed was auburn had dried, lightening to an incredible shade of strawberry blond that fell in a tangle of curls to the middle of her back. He couldn't think of one woman in his circle of friends who would let her hair grow to that length. Especially Amanda, who scheduled her six-week appointments at a trendy salon a year in advance.

But then again, he couldn't think of anyone who'd wear what looked like a man's dress shirt and jeans to an interview, either.

Cade frowned. Maybe Meghan McBride didn't realize that although Parker had hired her, he had the final say as to whether or not she *stayed* hired.

Without turning around, Meghan knew the exact second Cade walked into the kitchen. And it wasn't because of the subtle, musky scent of his cologne or the husky "good morning" he growled at Bert.

It was because the skin on her arms prickled.

She had goose bumps.

And Meghan *never* got goose bumps.

Rattled, Meghan scanned the counter for the pancake turner but couldn't remember what she'd done with it.

"It's in your apron pocket," Cade said helpfully.

Meghan opened her mouth to argue that she wouldn't put a cooking utensil in her pocket, but glanced down first, just in case he was right. And he was. Why did she get the feeling that Cade Halloway was always right?

Bert cruised past with a platter of hash browns and scrambled eggs, pausing long enough to flip on the fan in the hood above the range. "All set, Meghan?"

Meghan nodded, even though she was pretty sure she wouldn't be able to eat a bite of Bert's fabulous breakfast.

Once they were seated, every time Cade's unnerving cobalt gaze settled on her across the table, she knew he was silently questioning her qualifications. She refilled her plate—frequently—because basic etiquette said it was impolite for a person to talk with their mouth full.

"I can help you clean up, Bert." It would buy her a few extra minutes before Cade's interrogation…Meghan swiftly amended that negative thought…*interview*. That's what it was. An interview.

"Don't be silly. What else do I have to do?" Bert made a shooing motion with her hands. "Cade wants to talk to you and he's not the kind of man who likes to be kept waiting."

Meghan had figured that much out for herself. She hated to make snap judgments about people, but it was Saturday morning and Cade had dressed as if he were on his way to the office. The only thing missing was a conservative silk tie.

So maybe he *had* been blessed with traffic-stopping good looks but he was so…serious. The only time she'd seen the hint of a smile soften his features was when Bert had reminded him that it was *his* turn to catch their supper.

At least if she had to meet with Cade, it would give her an opportunity to pay more attention to the paintings hanging on the library walls.

She took a deep breath and tried to work up a smile.

"Come in, Miss McBride."

She would have, if she hadn't frozen in the doorway. How in the world did Cade manage to lower the temperature in a room as welcoming as the library? Instead of taking one of the chairs by the fireplace like he'd done the night before, he'd positioned himself at an antique secretary to conduct his interrog— *interview*.

"You can call me Meghan." Because it would be harder to fire her if they were on a first-name basis. Wouldn't it?

Cade's eyes narrowed.

Okay, maybe not.

He motioned to a chair but Meghan decided *not* to sit down. It would give him too much of an advantage. Instead she took a casual lap around the perimeter of the room to check out the artwork, sucking in a breath at the some of the signatures she saw. Nina Bonnefield hadn't been exaggerating when she'd told Patrick that the Halloway family supported the arts.

She was used to seeing paintings of this caliber displayed behind a satin rope in a museum or in an upscale gallery, not in a casual arrangement on a backdrop of sun-faded wallpaper.

Her stomach knotted at the sudden realization that maybe there *was* a Ferris somewhere on the premises.

"…found you."

Cade's voice filtered into her thoughts and snagged her attention. Meghan mentally kicked herself for getting lost in the paintings. "I'm sorry. What did you say?"

He frowned slightly. "Maybe we should start with how my sister…found you."

Found her? As if she were a stray cat?

Meghan bit down on her lower lip to prevent a smile. She'd already rehearsed the answer to this question. Her parents had taught her that honesty was the best policy and she'd made a promise to herself—and Ms. Bonnefield—that she wouldn't tell a lie to explain her presence on Blue Key Island.

"The usual way. By referral. An acquaintance of mine heard your sister was looking for a photographer…someone who didn't mind coming this far off the beaten path for a wedding."

He couldn't argue with that, now could he? Not only was Blue Key Island way off the beaten path, a person had to take a boat to get there. And she wasn't even charging them for mileage.

Cade's fingers drummed against the top of the desk. "What studio are you employed with?"

The knot in Meghan's stomach tightened. "I'm a free-lance photographer."

"Freelance." Cade repeated the word as if he'd never heard of it.

"That's right. I have my own business."

"Really."

It didn't escape Meghan's notice that Cade's sentences had gotten shorter as the interview progressed.

"I apprenticed with a master photographer for two years before opening my own studio five years ago." Which she ran out of her apartment, but Cade didn't need to know that. As her reputation had spread, she'd begun to travel more frequently but still tried to keep regular business hours.

"But you specialize in weddings."

It sounded more like a statement than a question, but since Cade seemed to be waiting for some sort of response, Meghan gave him a truthful one. "I take pictures of a variety of subjects." *And please don't ask what they are.*

"I'm sure my sister asked for references." Cade's fingers drummed against the top of the desk again.

Meghan simply smiled. She'd never met Parker Halloway in person and she had no idea if Parker had checked out her Web site. If she had, she would have discovered Meghan McBride *did* photograph a variety of subjects. Most of them just happened to have four legs. And occasionally, feathers.

Cade's eyes met hers and Meghan did her best not to flinch under the cool appraisal. "My sister can be a little… impulsive but she is a stickler for details. When you come back this weekend for the wedding—"

"Come back?" Meghan interrupted without thinking.

"It's only Saturday," Cade reminded her. "Parker and the rest of the wedding party won't arrive until Friday morning. I assumed you came to check things out today…."

And then leave.

Meghan silently filled in the rest of the sentence Cade Halloway was too polite to finish.

Now what? She needed a legitimate reason to explain her extended stay on the island and not compromise her promise to stick to honesty.

The cry of a loon filtered through the open window and with a flash of inspiration, Meghan found her reason. "I know I'm here early, but I happen to be free this week." Also the truth. "I'd love to photograph some of the wildlife."

The lean fingers on *both* of the man's hands made a series of tapping noises. Meghan realized Cade Halloway didn't vent his emotions. He "drummed" them instead. "I have a lot of work to do. I thought I'd be alone on the island before the wedding chaos started."

What a coincidence. She'd thought the same thing!

"You won't even know I'm here," Meghan added. In spite of his words, she sensed him weakening.

"Somehow I doubt that," Cade said under his breath.

The telephone suddenly rang, saving Meghan from having to respond. Cade reached for it with a terse, "Excuse me," and Meghan took that as a cue their interview was officially concluded.

She slipped out of the library, quietly closed the door and collapsed against the wall.

The Ferris was somewhere in the house.

Cade Halloway was in the house.

Meghan decided it was going to be a very long week.

Chapter Four

Meghan grabbed her camera—just in case Cade saw her—and stepped outside. Into wonderland.

Why hadn't she seen this the day before?

Probably because the pelting rain had forced her to keep her head down. And because she'd been so taken with the house, she'd failed to notice the yard.

Meghan took a hesitant step forward and paused, not sure where to begin. The strange silhouettes she'd seen in the shadows while she'd tripped along after Cade Halloway came to life in the bright morning sun. *Sculptures*. But not the kind a person found in the gardening section of the local discount store.

Meghan's gaze settled on a blue heron created out of angle iron and followed the elegant arch of its neck to the unblinking marble eye and the fish trapped in its beak.

To the right of the heron, a trio of baby raccoons clung to the trunk of a birch tree—their mother perched on a sturdy branch above them. They'd been soldered together with bits and pieces of discarded metal, but each of their masked faces somehow conveyed a different expression.

Automatically, Meghan's feet moved toward a bald eagle, hewn right from the stump of the tree it sat on, poised for flight.

Incredible.

Some of the sculptures were larger than life, but others, like the whimsical turtle made from a clam shell that peeked out from under the broad leaves of a hosta, were so small a person could walk right by and not notice them.

They not only differed in size, they differed in design. Some were primitive, a simple sketch of an animal or bird created with minimal materials, while others were so detailed they looked as if they were about to come to life right in front of her eyes.

She'd studied the works of Joseph Ferris in the car on the way to Willoughby and wondered if she was within reach of one of his creations. Ferris had worked in several mediums but seemed to favor watercolor. And although he'd been a product of the pop art culture of the sixties, he'd been more influenced by the early Impressionists. Meghan guessed that was the reason why his work had gone unnoticed until after his death.

She wandered through the sculpture garden, looking for something that reflected the spare lines and luminous colors Ferris favored.

"Amazing, isn't it?"

Meghan, who'd dropped to her knees to peer at a stained-glass replica of a dragonfly, started at the sound of a voice behind her.

"I didn't see any of this yesterday." Meghan's heart resumed its natural rhythm and she smiled up at Bert, who stood several feet away with Miss Molly nestled comfortably in the crook of her arm. "And I'm not sure *amazing* describes it." She reached out to pick up the dragonfly and then changed her mind. Maybe *someone* had instigated a No Touch rule.

"Go ahead."

"Are you sure?" Without thinking, Meghan glanced toward the house.

"I'm sure." Bert's low laugh told Meghan she'd guessed the reason behind her hesitation. "Besides, the dragonfly is one of mine."

Meghan picked it up and cradled it in the palm of her hand. "You're an artist?"

"I work with stained glass."

"It's beautiful."

Bert's eyes sparkled at the compliment. "I have a few minutes. I'll take you on a little tour of the island and show you the rest."

"There's more?"

A mysterious smile touched Bert's lips. "Oh, there's more."

Cade put down the phone and blew out a sigh, wondering if a photo of his aunt Judith was being faxed to every landscaping business in the county. He couldn't find anyone willing to come to the island and fix up the grounds before the wedding.

He walked over to the window but found his view almost completely obstructed by a hedge of fragrant arbor vitae desperately in need of a trim.

Without warning, a memory of his mother kneeling on a folded beach towel in the garden returned. While he and Parker had spent summer afternoons fishing for perch or catapulting themselves off the end of the dock, Genevieve had turned the island into an eclectic hodgepodge of gardens and objects d'art. A direct contrast to the formal decor of their house in Minneapolis.

He and Parker had grown up rattling around their father's childhood home in a neighborhood where the air still carried the faint whiff of "old money." Aunt Judith's influence had prevailed even there in the subdued neutrals and the furnishings arranged with museumlike perfection. Genevieve didn't so much as rearrange the jade statues on the mantel above the fireplace, but when Douglas purchased the island she'd practically designed the entire house, decorating it with airy fabrics and bright colors.

In Minneapolis, dinner guests were chosen from his father's business associates and potential clients; the conversation around the table as carefully planned as the menu. On the island, people dropped by with no advance notice and stayed as long as they wanted.

Judith had visited Blue Key only once that Cade could remember. She'd hated the water and the sand, declaring the place a tasteless "amusement park." And she'd never set foot on the island again.

Cade, who'd sensed the tension between his aunt and his mother even as a child, had a hunch Judith's refusal to visit Blue Key was fine with his mother. In fact, it suddenly occurred to him that Genevieve had smiled and laughed more when they were on the island than she had in her own home.

The carousel just beyond the concrete fountain in the center of the courtyard was a testimony to Genevieve's unusual taste. The painted horses had faded and patches of rust stained the metal canopy like a bad rash, but Cade remembered his mother's excitement when she'd discovered it during one of her frequent trips to the salvage yard.

The next time they'd visited the island, there it was.

He'd spent hours playing on it—the horse he "rode" reflecting the adventure he'd chosen to pursue at that particular moment in time. When he wanted to be a cowboy, he jumped on the brown bronco with wild eyes and a lasso painted over the saddle horn. If he was a knight, it was the black horse with its armored headpiece and sword.

Parker always claimed the white horse with a flowing mane and tail. The garland of roses around its neck hinted it was a derby winner, but from Cade's boyish perspective, flowers were flowers and he wasn't going to have anything to do with them.

All the horses were carved out of wood, the paint on the saddles and bridles original. As a piece of American history, the carousel must have been worth a fortune, but Genevieve had let him and Parker scramble on it as if it had been purchased from the back lot of a discount store.

Cade shook his head, not sure why they hadn't gotten rid of the thing years ago. Maybe he could donate it to one of the local museums. He'd been right to come back before listing with a Realtor. The rusted sculpture garden and the unusual objects his mother had collected might detract from the aesthetic value of the property.

He was turning away from the window when he caught a sudden movement out of the corner of his eye. Bert rounded the corner of the house with Meghan one step behind her.

Meghan's chirp of surprise must have had something to do with the carousel because she made a beeline directly over to it. With a delighted smile, she ran her hands up the white horse's face and over its mane as if it were real.

Cade knew he shouldn't be spying but stood there, riveted in place, as Meghan hoisted herself onto its back and wrapped her arms around its neck.

He winced as the camera, hanging by a cord around her neck, slammed against the horse's chest, but it didn't seem to faze her. He would have thought a photographer would be a little more careful with the most important tool of her trade.

When Bert slipped between the horses and fished around inside the mechanical box, Cade's shoulders tensed.

He doubted the thing worked after so many years. Even as a kid, he'd thought the simple tune the carousel played sounded muffled and rather tinny. Like the song a jack-in-the-box played right before a clown popped out of the top.

After a few minutes Bert gave up and Meghan slid off the horse's back. And headed toward the mermaid fountain. Another one of his mother's salvage-yard finds that had found its way to the island.

Maybe that was why no one in Willoughby would talk to him, Cade thought sourly. No doubt the old-timers remembered having to transport his mother's purchases to the island by fishing boat.

"…it work?" Meghan's lilting voice drifted through the screen as she started to scoop handfuls of wet leaves out of the fountain and drop them on the ground.

The fountain. Cade shook his head. One more reason to talk Parker out of her crazy idea to hold the wedding ceremony and reception on the island. Without an army of landscapers to tackle years of neglect, the place would never be ready for guests by the following weekend.

And Parker would have a fit if she saw the state the house and grounds were in. No doubt she still carried the memories of the way it was when they were children—not realizing Douglas had forbidden Bert to do anything other than the simplest maintenance projects in the house.

Cade still didn't understand why Bert had stayed on. He

knew Bert and his mother had been close friends. "Twins separated at birth" was the way Genevieve laughingly introduced Bert to visitors to the island. When he'd asked Douglas why Bert had stayed, his father had brushed aside the question in his typical gruff manner and muttered something about Bert not having anywhere else to go.

That didn't surprise Cade, since Bert belonged to the group of artists that Genevieve had counted as friends. What surprised him was his father's benevolence. Especially since Douglas had completely wiped out any reminders of Genevieve.

After Cade's mother walked out on them, they'd simply continued on as if Genevieve had never been a part of their lives. Judith had moved into the suite of rooms in the east wing of their home and taken over the household.

And Cade had never seen his mother again.

The one time he'd gathered the courage to ask if she was coming back, the look of raw pain in his father's eyes had discouraged him from ever bringing up the subject again.

Aunt Judith however, hadn't been as silent with her opinions. There'd been anger, not pain, in her voice when she'd explained that Genevieve had found being a wife and mother too confining. That she'd gone back to the lifestyle she was more suited for.

Cade shook away the unwelcome memories that crowded in. The sooner he wrapped things up on the island, the sooner he could leave. All he had to do was convince Parker that without a landscape team working around the clock—for the next six months—Blue Key Island wouldn't be the romantic setting for the wedding of her dreams she imagined it would be.

Cade had never understood, given Douglas's keen business sense, why his father had held on to the island all these years. He'd seen the tax bills. Why keep shelling out money for a place they hadn't visited for years? When they needed a getaway, they took advantage of their ownership in a luxury time-share.

He'd make sure Bert had a generous retirement package and close this particular chapter of Halloway history for good.

Selling the island was the logical solution.

Meghan couldn't believe Cade wanted to sell the island.

Everywhere she turned she saw evidence that the house and the surrounding grounds had been, at one time, someone's pride and joy.

A fountain, complete with a mermaid perched regally on a pearl inside an algae-stained oyster shell, created the centerpiece of the courtyard. Layers of decaying leaves filled the bowl instead of water and the rusty spout looked as if it hadn't been used in years, but the fountain hadn't lost its charm.

And even though grass had pushed its way through gaps in the stone footpaths and weeds vied with overgrown beds of perennials for sun and soil, when Meghan looked closely she could still see the outline of the garden's original design.

And an honest-to-goodness *carousel* stood in the shade of a sugar maple. She still couldn't get over that.

Meghan unearthed a green penny from the bottom of the fountain and scraped off a thin layer of slime with her thumbnail.

"Did you find something?" Bert asked.

Meghan held out the penny. "Someone forgot their wish."

Bert's smile was pensive as she took the coin from Meghan's hand. "I'm afraid there are a lot of those in there."

"It's such a shame—" Meghan bit back the rest of the sentence. She liked Bert and didn't want the woman to think she was being critical. It would have been impossible for one person to keep up with the maintenance required for a piece of property the size of Blue Key Island.

"Things are in such disrepair?" Bert finished the sentence for her.

"I didn't mean—"

"Don't worry. I know you didn't," Bert interrupted. "Repairs to the house are the only ones I'm able to authorize. To tell you the truth, I'm more like a well-paid, permanent houseguest than a caretaker." There was no undercurrent of bitterness in Bert's tone, only a quiet resignation that wrenched Meghan's heart.

"You must love it here." Meghan did, and she'd only been on the island twenty-four hours.

A spark of humor extinguished the shadows in Bert's eyes. "I love it enough to put up with mosquitoes the size of hummingbirds and the weather. Which, by the way, the locals refer to as nine months of winter and three months of poor skiing."

"You don't get lonely?"

"I have a few close friends in Willoughby who make sure I don't become too much of a hermit. And, of course, I have Miss Molly for company." Bert gave the dog an affectionate cuddle before setting her down on one of the multicolored path stones. Miss Molly immediately bounded toward the house with a joyful bark.

Meghan and Bert exchanged a grin. It wasn't difficult to guess where she was off to.

"We'll let her keep Cade company while I show you the stone cottage."

"Stone cottage?"

"The old studio. Years ago, it was quite the gathering place for the writers and artists who came here for inspiration."

Meghan's heart picked up speed. Artists like Joseph Ferris? Nina Bonnefield's story about a friendship with the man didn't sound so far-fetched anymore.

They hiked almost the entire width of the island until the woods opened up to reveal a flat, grassy area ringed by a stand of birch trees. In the distance, the lake shimmered in a changing pattern of blues and silvers.

Other than a few loose shingles on the roof and the crumbled corners of the foundation, the stone cottage seemed to be in better shape than the main house.

Someone had painted the front door of the cottage with a checkerboard pattern in blue and yellow. A collection of wind chimes harmonized in the trees. Once again, Meghan was charmed by the whimsical decor and wondered who was responsible for it.

They walked past a rocking chair fashioned from willow branches and Meghan couldn't help reaching out and setting it in motion.

Bert caught her. "Maeve Burke made that chair. You've probably never heard of her, but she's a well-known ceramics artist now. She visited Blue Key as a graduate student, when she was still trying to decide if she should pursue a career in art."

Meghan *had* heard of her. Maeve Burke was a native of Minnesota and some of the more exclusive shops carried her designs. In fact, Meghan had splurged and bought Evie and Sam a set of Maeve's signature jade and cream glazed coffee mugs as a wedding gift.

The breeze carried the scent of mint and Meghan spotted it next to the door, planted in an old galvanized washtub along with clusters of parsley and chives spiked with lavender flowers.

"I broke the rules and keep the herb garden weeded," Bert confided. "I love to use them when I cook."

"You rebel." Meghan couldn't resist teasing the older woman.

Bert laughed. "Come in. I have a feeling you'll feel right at home in here."

She was right.

Paintings in a variety of sizes crowded the walls, creating a mural all their own. Meghan gravitated toward a large watercolor in a rustic driftwood frame. She recognized the boathouse where she'd taken refuge from the storm. And met Cade for the first time.

Instant goose bumps again.

What was that about? Meghan impatiently rubbed them away with her fingertips and scanned the corners of the painting until she spotted the artist's name. "Who is G.H.?"

"Genevieve Halloway." Bert walked over and stood beside her.

"Halloway?"

"My best friend. And Cade and Parker's mother."

Chapter Five

"She's very good." Meghan studied the muted colors and delicate brushstrokes.

"Yes." Bert's guarded tone sent a shiver of unease up Meghan's spine.

Now she had no doubt it was Cade's mother's influence she saw everywhere she looked. And she could think of no other reason for the obvious neglect other than Genevieve's… absence.

Bert must have seen the questions in her eyes. "After Genevieve left, Douglas got the island in the divorce settlement. He closed up the place to…visitors…and the family stopped spending summers here. Until Cade showed up a few days ago, I hadn't seen him since he was ten years old."

It explained a lot but left many questions unanswered. And raised a whole host of others. Like why hadn't Douglas ever returned to the island? And why hadn't Bert been forced into exile with the rest of Genevieve's friends? But, Meghan reasoned, if Nina Bonnefield had, it might explain why she didn't feel comfortable approaching the Halloway family about the gift Joseph Ferris had supposedly left behind for her.

"Genevieve loved Blue Key—I think she considered the island her real home. All the things you see—the gardens, the fountain, the carousel—they're here because of her. I still can't believe everything is going to be auctioned off."

Neither could Meghan. If Cade had spent his childhood summers on the island, why didn't he feel more of a connection to it?

She tried to make sense out of the bits and pieces Bert had shared. It sounded as though Genevieve had been the one who'd instigated the divorce. The house the Halloways loved had been closed up, no longer welcoming friends or providing a peaceful retreat for the family.

With a start, Meghan realized Bert had stopped talking. Probably because she'd noticed Meghan had stopped listening!

"I'm sorry," Meghan said simply. And she was. When Meghan was younger, she'd try to bluff her way through situations like this by smiling, nodding and making eye contact. Or by catching a few words that hadn't sifted through her thoughts and trying to *guess* what the person had just said.

Caitlin had put an end to that one day in her usual, no-nonsense way.

Megs, you zone out on people and they think they're boring you. And then they wonder if they're boring the rest of the world, too. If you lose track of the conversation, just say you're sorry and ask for a recap. Easy.

Not so easy, but Meghan had taken her advice. She didn't want anyone to think they were the reason she was distracted. That's why she preferred working with animals instead of people. Less pressure. They never seemed to mind if her thoughts jumped around or she lost her place in the middle of a conversation.

Growing up, Meghan had been described by her exasperated teachers as sweet, but also "dreamy" and "imaginative." They coaxed her to try harder. To pay attention. When she struggled to remember things she'd read and the lectures she heard, she'd wished she was smarter, like Caitlin and Evie. No matter how often she'd grit her teeth and force herself to concentrate, she had a difficult time staying focused on a task.

Although popular in school, Meghan began to withdraw from social situations where following multiple conversations became stressful and she was afraid people would notice something different about her and she'd be slapped with the "weird" label. Fortunately, her strengths were in the artistic, creative areas so being quirky was more acceptable, but she still couldn't count the number of times she'd heard the familiar greeting "earth to Meghan" uttered by her classmates. She'd laugh…and then stare up at the ceiling at night and cry, wondering why it was so easy to get lost in her own thoughts that she missed what was going on around her.

It wasn't until Meghan was in college that she'd found out she had Attention Deficit Disorder. And she had Evie to thank. Her sister, a high school freshman at the time, had stumbled on the signs of ADD while writing a research paper. For the first time, Meghan understood why she was the way she was. Accepting that ADD wasn't something that would go away, like a bad cold, wasn't as easy.

It had helped when Evie had started to refer to it as Attention Deficit *Design*. She'd carefully written out the verse from Psalm 139 and framed it for Meghan, reminding her that God had designed her and she was "fearfully and wonderfully made."

The day she'd hung it on the wall, Meghan had decided she was going to work with her strengths instead of wishing away what some would view as weaknesses.

Even now, seeing herself mirrored in Bert's friendly gaze, Meghan had to resist the urge to scold herself for letting her thoughts drift away.

"Woolgathering?" Bert smiled. "Don't apologize. I do that myself on occasion."

"Not just gathering," Meghan admitted. "Carding, spinning and turning into sweaters."

Bert laughed and linked her arm through Meghan's. "You remind me of an old friend."

Genevieve? Or maybe Nina Bonnefield?

Meghan was tempted to ask but her dad had made her promise, at Nina's request, that she wouldn't mention his client's name to anyone.

But that hadn't raised any red flags with Patrick. No, of course not.

At this point, Meghan had more questions than answers. Bert seemed to be familiar with the people who'd visited the island. It was possible the two women's paths had crossed. Maybe they'd even been friends. But if that was the case, why wouldn't Nina have contacted Bert directly about the Ferris?

The bottom line was that even though she liked Bert, she didn't know her—or the situation—well enough to disclose any more information. And Bert's first loyalty would be to her employer. Who also happened to have the power to fire Meghan if he took a notion.

"I'm going to start lunch soon, but we can take the long way back to the house, past the cabins," Bert said.

Meghan wanted more time to study the artwork in the

studio, but didn't want Bert to get suspicious. She decided to come back later. Alone.

She started to follow Bert when a trio of charcoal sketches, each showcasing the same tree but in a different season, caught her eye. "These aren't signed."

Bert paused. "That's not unusual. The artists who came here weren't under any pressure to produce something salable. Some of them needed a quiet place to think. To share ideas. Creative people find different ways to express themselves. Genevieve understood that. She put as much thought and effort into her gardens as she did in her paintings."

Meghan understood, too. Photography was her first love, but when she wasn't traveling or in the studio, she volunteered with Sidewalk Chalk, a citywide children's art ministry sponsored by local churches. Meghan didn't consider herself a painter, but she loved turning a wall or sidewalk into a mural that brought beauty to a color-hungry neighborhood.

With a sinking heart, she also realized that dozens of unsigned works scattered around the island would make it that much harder to identify an unsigned work by Joseph Ferris.

"I can't count the number of people who came here weary and burned out, but left the island refreshed."

Meghan wondered if that was because of the peaceful surroundings or the woman who'd welcomed them.

"Genevieve...she'll be here for the wedding, won't she?" Meghan had a sudden urge to meet the woman who'd turned an entire island into her own unique art gallery.

"I don't—"

"My mother has missed every milestone in Parker's life for the past twenty years. I doubt she'll break tradition and show up for this one."

Meghan pivoted and saw Cade standing in the doorway.

He had to stop sneaking up on her like that. *She* was supposed to be the one doing the sneaking.

Cade regretted the words as soon they came out of his mouth.

He had enough to do without sorting through the skeletons in the family closet. Especially in front of witnesses.

His eyes locked with Meghan's across the room and he saw a flash of compassion in their velvety-green depths. He looked away. Quickly. In the space of twenty-four hours, Meghan McBride had managed to set foot everywhere on the island he'd been trying to avoid.

He'd decided to talk to Bert about hiring a new landscaping crew, but by the time he'd walked around the house to the courtyard, she and Meghan had disappeared.

Miss Molly, who managed to get herself lost on a regular basis but had a knack for finding *him* at any given moment, had taken over the search. He'd hoped the cabins were her target, but she'd veered off the main path and charged toward the clearing, her destination obvious.

Cade hadn't meant to eavesdrop on their conversation, but they'd left the door standing wide open and he couldn't help overhearing part of it. Meghan and Bert were in Genevieve's studio, so it didn't surprise him to discover they'd been talking about his mother. What surprised him was the confidence in Meghan's tone when she brought up the wedding. As if there were no doubt that no matter what the circumstances, Genevieve, the mother of the bride, would be attending.

Because that's what a mother would do.

But not his mother.

As if it had taken place yesterday, he remembered the unsettling question Parker had asked him several days after Justin proposed. She'd stopped by the office to coax him into going out for lunch with her and Cade thought he knew what was on his sister's mind. Their aunt hadn't taken the news of Parker's engagement well and she needed him on her side. Judith had plans for her niece's future and none of them included her marrying a missionary with no assets or family connections.

It turned out, however, that Aunt Judith hadn't been the reason she'd wanted to talk to him. She'd waited until they were halfway through dessert before dropping the bomb on him.

Do you think I should let Mom know I'm engaged?

Cade's response had been an immediate *no*. Instead of getting angry or pouting, two tools Parker utilized on a regular basis for getting her way, she'd listened patiently until he'd run out of reasons. And even on such short notice, Cade had been able to come up with quite a few.

Parker hadn't argued with him—another unusual occurrence—and when he'd finally asked her why she'd even consider letting Genevieve know about the wedding, she told him it had been Justin's idea. Apparently her fiancé had strong feelings about lugging "personal baggage from the past" into their future.

Cade had dismissed the idea immediately. It was healthier for people to move forward than to constantly be looking back, trying to make sense of a past they couldn't change.

He'd never understood how their mother could simply walk away from her family and never contact them again, but *she'd* made the choice. And the hole Genevieve's absence had left had slowly closed over the years.

Cade didn't see the point of prying it open again.

Parker had changed the subject after he'd suggested she and Justin deal with any "baggage" during their premarital counseling sessions. But he'd still felt uneasy she'd brought it up at all.

The bottom line was, he didn't want his sister to get hurt. Or rejected. He and Parker were both adults now—if Genevieve wanted to get to know them, there was nothing to prevent her from contacting them. The fact she hadn't could only mean one thing. She didn't want to.

He couldn't remember Parker ever bringing up the subject of Genevieve. He had quite a few memories of her, but Parker, who'd only been six years old when Genevieve left, hadn't understood just what had fractured their family.

Cade envied her. Which was another reason why Parker needed to leave the past in the past...

"Did you need something, Cade?"

Bert's cautious question yanked him back to reality. Once again the past had derailed the present. He blamed Blue Key Island. "A landscaping crew."

"I thought Parker had lined one up."

"She did. But Aunt Judith must have gotten their phone number."

"Ah." Bert, who'd met Aunt Judith once and had probably never forgotten the experience, tried not to smile.

"I've been trying to get in touch with Parker to talk her into having the ceremony at the church instead."

"It's a little late to change the location now, isn't it?" Meghan blurted.

Cade gave her the Look. The one he used to put upstart summer interns in their place. It didn't seem to work on upstart wedding photographers. He gave in. "Until a few weeks ago, Parker and Justin had reserved the church for the wedding. It's probably still available."

"The church might work out, but what about the reception?" Bert frowned. "The country club is booked two years in advance. Especially for a July wedding. I doubt Parker is going to want to hold the reception in the fellowship hall of a church basement."

Cade doubted it, too. Parker had a reputation for wanting—and expecting—the best of the best. He still had a hard time believing his sister had willingly given up her "fairy-tale" wedding—Cade thought the description "high-budget production" more appropriate—to get married on the island. Aunt Judith was still fuming over that decision.

"If Parker saw this place, she'd agree the fellowship hall is more suitable." Cade heard a stifled gasp and arched an eyebrow in Meghan's direction. "Something to add, Miss McBride?"

"The island is *perfect* for the wedding and reception. My sister, Evie, just got married in an outdoor ceremony a few weeks ago at our father's home and it was beautiful."

"I'm sure it was. I'm also sure the lawn didn't look like the set from *Jurassic Park.*"

Meghan's chin lifted. "There has to be a lawn mower around here somewhere. Right, Bert?"

Bert made a choking sound. "Yes, there is."

"What are you suggesting?" He had a feeling he knew. He just wanted her to say it out loud.

"I'm *suggesting* we don't need a landscaping crew. I can pull a few weeds and mow the grass. Between, um, taking pictures of the loons."

He glanced at Bert and she shrugged, not even trying to hide her amusement.

"Tell her she'd be fighting a losing battle, Bert."

But the challenging gleam in the caretaker's eyes told Cade she was throwing her line in with Meghan. Her next words confirmed it. "I've wanted to give the courtyard a makeover for years."

Cade's brain began to break down the situation, organizing it into his usual list of pros and cons.

He was too busy to add anything else to his to do list. The auctioneer expected Cade's phone call by the end of the week to set up an appointment to inventory the contents of the main house. Cade had planned to have a detailed list of his own before then.

On the other hand, it probably *was* too late to find a suitable place for the reception….

"Great," Meghan said. "Can you show me where the gardening tools are, Bert?"

Cade frowned. Had he missed something? *Like saying yes?*

It occurred to him that working on the courtyard meant he'd be spending more time with Meghan.

Cade, whose logical brain always knew exactly where things fit, suddenly wasn't sure whether to file that on the "pro" side or the "con" side.

And why did he get the unsettling feeling that Meghan McBride was the kind of woman who demanded a column all of her own?

Chapter Six

What happened back there, Meghan? Did you or did you not just offer to perform manual, backbreaking labor free of charge? In between taking pictures of the loons?

Yes, she had.

And all because she'd stood up for a piece of property that didn't even belong to her.

Meghan pulled on the pair of leather gloves Bert had given her and surveyed the courtyard, not sure which section to wade into first.

It was all Cade Halloway's fault. If he hadn't said the island "wasn't suitable" for a wedding, she wouldn't have felt the need to express her opinion.

Not suitable.

Cade Halloway had *no* imagination.

Without closing her eyes, Meghan could picture luminaries hanging from the branches of the trees while the fountain provided the background music for the ceremony. If it still worked…and the carousel horses would wear garlands of real flowers around their necks.

Meghan couldn't think of a more beautiful spot for a couple in love to say their vows.

Too bad she knew as much about landscaping as she did about photographing weddings. And how was she supposed to find the Ferris when she'd be on her knees pulling weeds in the courtyard instead of doing her best Nancy Drew impression *inside* the house?

She had to make an emergency call to Caitlin. Caitlin not only had a gift for helping people make the most of what God had given them, she could apply that gift to just about anything. Cramped apartments. Messy closets—Meghan knew that firsthand—and cluttered desks—again, firsthand knowledge. Why not gardens?

She could take photos with her camera, send them off with an SOS and get some input from a professional.

Bert had offered to help, so it wasn't as if she were in this alone. She'd gone inside to make a salad for lunch but Meghan expected her back to provide moral—and trowel—support any minute now.

"Having second thoughts?"

Meghan's trowel clattered to the stones at the sound of Cade's voice and missed her foot by an inch. "Stop. Doing. That."

"Doing what?" He looked genuinely confused.

"Sneaking up on me."

Now he looked genuinely exasperated. "I didn't sneak up on you. You were lost in thought." A slow smile turned up the corners of his lips and worked its way to his eyes. "Or maybe regret."

The courtyard wasn't overwhelming. That smile was. It transformed his features, igniting a warm blue flame in his eyes and carving out a captivating indentation in his left cheek. One that would have been labeled a dimple on anyone else's face.

But whatever it was called, the sight of it sucked the air right out of Meghan's lungs.

She knelt down to retrieve the trowel. And give her voice a chance to recover. Her heart would have to catch up later.

"Are you sure you know what you're doing?" Cade asked.

"I'm going to start by pulling out everything that doesn't look like a flower." She pushed a confident note into her voice. The same one she'd used on the loan officer when she'd filled out the paperwork to open her studio five years ago.

"Fine by me. Let's go."

"Go where?" Panic shot through her. Another interrog… *interview?* To make sure she was qualified to pull weeds?

"I'll rephrase that," Cade said patiently. "Let's get started."

For the first time, Meghan spotted the garden tool in his hand.

"You're—" Meghan gulped. "Going to…*help?*"

The crease in his cheek made another brief but memorable appearance. "Two are better than one, for they have a good return for their work."

"You took my verse." Meghan couldn't believe he remembered it. And quoted it. Verbatim. Was it possible Cade Halloway was a…believer?

Or did he just have a good memory?

"I surrender." Bert swept off her white straw hat and waved it above her head. "The weeds win this round. At least for today. I should spend some time in the studio while the natural light is still good."

Meghan sat back on her heels and blotted the moisture

from her forehead with the back of her glove, surveying the small section of garden stones she'd been clearing. The three of them had been working for close to three hours, stopping only for a light lunch, and they'd barely made a difference.

She glanced at Cade under her lashes, waiting for him to say *I told you so.* And knowing she probably deserved it.

Lord, I think you should assign a crossing guard to me instead of a guardian angel. Someone who will yell STOP if I'm about to get myself into trouble.

Meghan smiled at the thought, knowing God understood its origins. Her sisters did claim she had a tendency to leap before she looked. Meghan preferred to think of it as exercising her faith.

But in this instance, maybe even she'd been overly optimistic. Not that she'd lost her vision of how the courtyard *could* look after some TLC. Okay, a *lot* of TLC. The challenge was getting it to that point in time for Parker Halloway's wedding.

Meghan's heart locked up when her eyes met Cade's across the courtyard. One eyebrow arched in a silent question and Meghan realized she was still smiling.

She looked away, breaking the connection.

Even with that slightly arrogant eyebrow, Cade Halloway was downright dangerous to her peace of mind. Here she'd been ready to dismiss him as the poster boy for the serious, alpha executive, not knowing there was a smile lurking below the surface capable of short-circuiting every neuron in her body.

When they'd set to work, she'd quickly discovered Cade was a dedicated multitasker who could pull weeds *and* conduct part two of his interview. The one she'd thought she'd successfully survived that morning.

Apparently not.

Oh, he'd been subtle. This time his questions had come under the guise of making friendly conversation. A barrage of questions was difficult enough to process—Meghan had to sort through them all and hope none of them slipped through the cracks—but screening them first to make sure she didn't blow her cover was even more stressful.

When had her interest in photography started? Where was her studio located? How many weddings did she usually photograph during a summer?

The first question had been easy. Meghan had always been the designated family photographer but didn't realize she had a knack for it until the yearbook adviser encouraged her to come on board her sophomore year of high school. She didn't bother to mention the peace and quiet of the dark room relaxed her. She even loved the sour smell of the chemicals. But most of all, she loved seeing the photographs, amazing moments of *life* captured in time, developed in the trays right in front of her eyes.

Cade Halloway struck her as a just-the-facts, give-me-an-answer-in-ten-words-or-less kind of guy. Kind of like Evie's Sam, except her brother-in-law's frequent smiles were warm and easygoing. Cade's sense of humor, if he had one, was hidden as well as the Ferris she was searching for.

She'd seen the flash of disbelief in his eyes when she'd reluctantly relayed the address of her studio. And even though loyalty to her quaint but underappreciated neighborhood had immediately surfaced, she'd resisted the urge to defend it. Her aching knees reminded her of what had happened the last time she'd attempted to defend a piece of property.

Fortunately, Bert had appeared, saving Meghan from having to answer his last question. Which would have been *none.* Unless she counted the German shepherd, dressed in a tuxedo, which she'd photographed for a "faithful friends" calendar the month before.

Meghan had taken advantage of Bert's presence and offered to help her clear another section of stones. Far enough away from Cade that he couldn't talk to her without shouting.

Interview over. Meghan had breathed a sigh of relief when Cade had turned his attention to the fountain. And away from her.

They'd all worked in relative silence until Bert had made her weary announcement and "surrendered."

"I've got some phone calls to make, too." Cade stood up, his lean frame unfolding with the fluid grace of a natural athlete.

Meghan guessed tennis. Or golf. Bert had mentioned the country club. Wasn't that where wealthy, successful businessmen kept in shape and networked?

He and Bert were both looking at her now and Meghan took the hint.

"I'll take a break, too," she said. It wasn't that she didn't want to. She just wasn't sure her cramped muscles would cooperate and she didn't want to fall flat on her face in front of Cade.

"Help yourselves to some lemonade. And there are sugar cookies in the jar by the coffeepot. I'll be back in time to make supper. That is, if Cade catches something for us to eat." Bert shaded her eyes against the sun, judged its strength and set off in the direction of the studio.

And just like that, they were alone again. Meghan didn't count Miss Molly, who'd spent the last few hours napping next to Cade.

"I forgot I was supposed to catch supper." Cade scrubbed

a hand over his jaw. "What are the chances of Louie's Shrimp Shack delivering this far?"

Meghan laughed, surprised he knew about the humble little seafood restaurant slouched on the corner of a street not far from where she lived. "I doubt it. And Bert might be suspicious when you bring her the fish already breaded and in a little white box."

"Good point." Cade continued to stare at her until Meghan began to wonder if she had a smear of dirt on her cheek.

Please, Lord, I can't take round three of the interview!

"What are your plans for the rest of the afternoon?"

To stay as far away from you as I can. "I'm going to scout out some places on the island that might make good photo ops." Because that's what the wedding photographer would be expected to do.

At the mention of the wedding, a shadow skimmed across Cade's face. "If I were you, I'd pass up any place that involves sand, water and anything my sister might step in or trip over in high heels."

Meghan's lips parted, but she didn't have time to form a comment before Cade muttered a terse see-you-later, snapped his phone open and strode away. A man on a mission.

Well, she had a mission, too. And it was time she started focusing on that mission instead of wondering what it would take to coax out that fascinating dent in Cade Halloway's cheek again.

"I'm sorry. The connection is bad…I can't hear you very well." Cade managed to catch two words before static choked off the rest of them.

I quit.

Bliss Markham, wedding coordinator extraordinaire, had apparently become the next casualty in Aunt Judith's war on the wedding plans.

Who was next? The cleaning crew?

If that was the case, Meghan would expect him to wash windows and sweep out those old relics...*cabins*...when what they really needed was a match.

A smile tugged at the corner of Cade's lips and he shook his head.

He still couldn't believe she'd talked him into letting her and Bert clean up the courtyard. He wasn't sure what had tipped the balance in Meghan's favor. Had it been the sudden image of the way the courtyard had once looked or the stubborn tilt of Meghan's chin when she defended it?

Not that it mattered. He could predict what would happen. They'd spend hours working in the hot sun and Parker would burst into tears upon arrival.

He knew his sister. Even if a professional landscape design team took on the grounds, they wouldn't meet her high standards.

Even though he was still a little taken aback by the changes he'd seen in his sister since she'd met Justin, Cade put them down to her wanting to make a good impression on the man she loved.

Parker had started planning her wedding long before she'd had a serious boyfriend. If Cade wasn't mistaken, she'd started dreaming about it in the sixth grade. By the time she graduated from high school, she had a folder bulging with pictures of satin gowns, wedding cakes and flower arrangements.

So what was she trying to prove, changing the location from the country club chapel to Blue Key Island? And would it make a difference if she knew her wedding planner, the woman she'd hired to take care of all the details, had jumped ship?

There was one way to find out.

Cade punched in the code for Parker's cell but the call went directly to her voice mail.

Parker only rerouted her calls for two reasons. If she was doing some serious shoe shopping or if she was hiding. And if Judith had called Parker half the amount of times she'd tried to call him in the past few hours, Cade guessed she was hiding.

He buried a sigh and looked down at Miss Molly, who'd sprawled across his foot during his conversation with Bliss Markham.

"I guess we don't have any more excuses. If we want something to eat for supper, we better go fishing."

As if she understood every word, Miss Molly bounced to her feet and bolted toward the house without a backward glance. Letting him know in no uncertain terms that fishing was strictly a pastime for humans.

"Fine. Be that—" Way. Cade groaned. He was talking to a *dog*. Now he knew the heat was getting to him. Or maybe it was the island.

When he was young, he'd thought Blue Key was the most magical place in the world. And his mother had encouraged the notion by scattering odd little collectibles around the island.

It hadn't been unusual for Cade to go exploring and discover hidden treasures. A metal chest filled with smooth stones. Animals, sculpted from wood and metal, peering at him from the brush. An old pocket watch or an arrowhead nestled in the notch of a tree, waiting to be found.

He'd hunt down Genevieve and pull her along, anxious to show her what he'd found. The delight on her face always looked genuine—as if, Cade thought cynically, the things he'd discovered hadn't been strategically planted for him to find.

Someday you'll bring your family here and you can tell your sons and daughters that this is a place where dreams come true.

Cade's jaw tightened at the memory.

By fall, Genevieve was gone. And Cade didn't remember the island as a place where dreams came true. He remembered it as the place they'd fallen apart.

Chapter Seven

Meghan eased the door open and slipped inside the library.

The thud of her heart threatened to drown out the quiet, methodical tick of the grandfather clock in the corner and she forced herself to take a deep breath.

Cade had taken the boat out and Bert was in the studio. It was a golden opportunity to have the house to herself to look for the Ferris.

Meghan paused in front of a group of paintings and checked the signatures. All of them were signed but none with the signature she hoped to see. She shifted her attention to a watercolor of a boat anchor half buried in the sand. Instantly she recognized it as one of Genevieve Halloway's.

Once again the attention to detail, right down to the single seagull feather ruffled by an unseen breeze, amazed her. And made her wonder about Cade's mother all over again.

She hadn't missed the touch of bitterness in Cade's voice when he'd told her Genevieve had missed all the important milestones in Parker's life.

And in his.

Meghan closed her eyes briefly as memories pressed against an old wound, resurrecting a familiar ache.

Every time she and her sisters had huddled together to make wedding plans, Meghan felt the weight of their mother's absence and wished she could have been there with them.

Meghan had been a freshman in college when Laura McBride, a police sergeant, was killed while assisting a stranded motorist during a storm. She could still remember the exact moment she'd gotten the phone call from Caitlin. Five-seventeen. She'd curled up on the bed in her dorm room and stared at the clock. Everything inside of her had frozen solid but the clock kept ticking away the minutes. Pushing her forward into a life without Laura McBride's wisdom and loving guidance.

She'd learned that night that life is as short as it is precious and she couldn't understand how some families allowed things like misunderstandings, unforgiveness…or even in-difference…to steal away the time they had.

No matter how bitter the Halloways' divorce had been or the circumstances behind it, Meghan couldn't imagine Gene-vieve walking out of her children's lives. Not being there for birthdays and graduations. Or her only daughter's wedding.

She reached out and traced the picture frame with the tip of her finger.

It didn't make sense. Everywhere Meghan looked, she saw evidence of a woman who had been nurturing. Someone who saw beauty in the unexpected and generously shared her home with people who needed a place to rest.

Genevieve Halloway still has time to reconnect with her family, Lord. They can start over. There isn't anything broken that you can't put back together. It's not too late. Can't you somehow show them that?

Whatever had happened, Meghan believed it wasn't beyond God's reach. Nothing was.

The grandfather clock began to chime the hour, a reminder she had more rooms to search before Bert—*or Cade*—returned.

Ten more minutes convinced her that none of the paintings in the library were by Joseph Ferris.

Meghan stepped back into the hall and hesitated, not sure where to go next. Upstairs or downstairs?

Her bedroom was on the second floor, so she'd have more opportunities to look around up there without making anyone suspicious.

Downstairs it was, Meghan decided.

She bypassed the kitchen and half bath and headed down to the end of the narrow hall. Door number one, two or three? Cade was staying in one of the rooms but she wasn't sure which one.

She nudged the first door open and breathed a sigh of relief. Once upon a time, this room must have been Parker's.

Airy dotted Swiss curtains trimmed with white pompoms welcomed the sunlight and the walls had been painted a delicate seashell-pink. Twin iron beds, covered by matching comforters, flanked the oak wardrobe like bookends.

Meghan took a quick lap around the room, pausing in front of each picture. All the artwork on the walls was dried-flowers or leaves, carefully preserved under glass.

She ducked out again and closed the door, mentally crossing Parker's room off her list. Evie would be proud to know she actually had a list.

She probably had time to search one more room.

Meghan's heart bunched up when she peeked inside the next room and saw the expensive leather case at the foot of the bed.

Somehow she would have expected Cade to choose the master suite that overlooked the sculpture garden.

Meghan would have backed right out of the room if she hadn't spotted a small painting of a rowboat hanging above the headboard.

Her heart picked up speed as she padded into the room, her eyes fixed on the painting. Ferris had done several paintings of boats on the water using the same sparse style.

Her gaze traced the silhouette of the man sitting in the boat, his face lifted toward the sky. The soft play of light on the horizon hinted it was either dawn or just after sunset. Obviously the artist left that to the imagination of the person looking at the painting.

She swallowed hard and looked at the corner. No signature.

With trembling fingers, she lifted the painting off the wall to see if there was a name on the back of the canvas.

"What do you think you're doing?"

Megan almost dropped the painting as she whirled around and her eyes met Cade's. "I…"

A movement in between the pillows grabbed their attention and Miss Molly poked her head up, a sock dangling from her mouth. Her ears perked up at the sight of Cade standing in the doorway.

"Ah…Miss Molly," Meghan said, hoping, praying, those two words would explain her presence.

"I wondered where she disappeared." Cade's eyes rolled toward the ceiling before coming to rest meaningfully on the painting still clutched in Meghan's hands.

"I…was curious who did this."

"Why?" The word came out like a single shot and blew Meghan's confidence to bits.

Meghan looked at Miss Molly, who wasn't inclined to rescue her a second time. "The light…the way the man is looking up at the sky instead of the water. It almost looks as if he's…praying—"

"Don't bother looking. It isn't signed."

"Oh." Meghan moistened her lips. Would Cade know if Ferris was the artist? "Do you know who did it?"

Cade hesitated a fraction of a second. "I did."

"I…*you* painted this? I didn't know you were an artist." Meghan looked down at the canvas and then at Cade, still frozen in the doorway. "Where do you show your work?"

"I don't. I'm not an artist, I'm an architect." Cade stalked into the room. Which suddenly felt a lot smaller as he entered the perimeter of her personal space.

"But this is the way you express yourself." Meghan smiled, warmth stirring inside her at this unexpected glimpse into Cade's personality.

"I express myself in my *work*," Cade said sharply. "And just so we're clear, I painted that when I was ten years old and I haven't picked up a brush since then."

He plucked the painting from her nerveless fingers and tossed it casually onto the bed. It landed upside down. Meghan would have rescued it but something in the tempered blue flame of Cade's eyes warned her not to.

"Ten years…" Meghan's voice trailed off. Impossible. If he possessed this kind of talent, someone would have encouraged it. Helped him refine it. "But how could you…stop?"

Cade stilled. When he spoke, his voice was soft. "I didn't stop because I never *started*. I painted a picture on a rainy afternoon when I was bored. That's it."

Meghan refused to believe that was it. If a ten-year-old boy could capture such raw emotion with no formal training, where would he be now if he'd pursued it as a career? "But you have a gift."

"A gift." Cade repeated the words. "Do you know how many people I met on this island with that gift? But looking back, I doubt any of them could have come up with a month's rent, let alone support themselves. Or a family. It's a self-centered, reckless pursuit that I'd call a burden, not a gift."

"Sometimes a gift does feel like a burden," Meghan admitted, remembering the sleepless nights and countless hours she'd spent on her knees, asking God if she should start her own business. Even now, the path wasn't always smooth but Meghan couldn't imagine the alternative. Following her dream had deepened her relationship with God in ways she'd never expected. With every stumbling step forward, the faith in knowing she was pursuing the seed of a dream *God* had planted inside her had given her the strength and courage to take the next one. "But if it's there inside of you and you ignore it—or give it up—you take on another kind of burden."

An emotion Meghan couldn't quite define flickered in Cade's eyes. "Not many artists are successful enough to make a living."

"Maybe some of them think it's more important to make a life," Meghan said quietly. Reaching for the painting, she stretched up on her tiptoes and hung it back on the wall.

Stepping back, Meghan realized that in the few seconds it took her to align the frame against the faded square on the wall, Cade had left the room.

Cade's hands clenched at his sides as he retreated down the hall.

A dreamer. No wonder she seemed right at home on Blue Key. The island had been tailor-made for people like her.

His instincts about Meghan McBride were right. He should have known they were right when she'd reluctantly told him the address of her studio. His firm's monthly utility bill was probably higher than the rent in the run-down neighborhood where Meghan's business was located. She must be barely making ends meet if she couldn't afford office space that didn't come equipped with bars on the windows to keep the non-paying customers out!

If Meghan had attained any level of success in the five years she'd been on her own, the first thing she would have done was rent space in a better part of the city. The fact she didn't meant that she couldn't afford to. Which meant she was struggling. And the term "struggling artist" had been coined for a reason.

Cade cut into the library and tossed his cell phone on the desk, still rattled by the conversation.

But how could you stop?

It was the last question he'd expected Meghan to ask. And the last one he wanted to answer.

He might have some artistic ability but with his father's encouragement, he'd used it to pave the way to a lucrative career.

Why spend your life doodling in sketchbooks no one will see when you can design buildings? You'll have something to show for all your hard work at the end of the day and money in the bank.

During Cade's adolescent and teenage years, Douglas Halloway's favorite lecture had gradually drowned out Genevieve's gentle encouragement to follow his heart. As a child, he hadn't understood what that meant. But now he did. It was an excuse people used when they selfishly went after what they wanted without caring what—or who—they left behind.

His cell phone rang, jarring him out of the past.

"Cade?" His name was barely audible through the snap, crackle and pop in the background.

"Parker? I've been trying to get in touch with you all morning." Cade's frustration leaked out in his voice. "Why haven't you been answering your phone? The landscape crew quit. And so did your wedding planner—"

"Her name is Bliss Markham…should be there tomorrow afternoon. I'm so glad you're on the island. Homeland security, you know." Parker giggled at her own joke.

Giggled.

"This is Parker, isn't it?" Suddenly Cade wasn't sure. "And did you hear what I said? The island won't be ready for a wedding this weekend." It wouldn't be ready for a wedding by *next* summer. "You're going to have to come up with another plan."

"What? I can barely hear you. Justin says hello, by the way." Another giggle.

Parker was twenty-six years old. Way past the giggling phase. Cade's back teeth ground together. "Tell him hello." He tried another tack. "Meghan McBride showed up yesterday."

"Meghan who?"

"McBride. Your wedding photographer." *The one I found asleep in the boathouse. Strawberry blond hair. Misty-green eyes.*

"That might be her name. A friend of a friend recommended her."

Cade frowned. "You didn't check her references yourself?"

"Listen…fading out. I'll call you tomorrow. Bliss has everything under control so I'm not worried…"

"Wait a second, Parker. Bliss—"

Call lost.

Quit.

Cade plowed his hand through his hair and then hit redial. The call went right to voice mail.

"Parker…call me back. Now." Cade growled.

Ten minutes later, he gave up.

Parker wanted a wedding to remember. Cade had a feeling his sister was going to get her wish.

He'd have to call Judith and ask her to get the message about Bliss Markham to Parker. He hated to involve his aunt, but he didn't want his sister's wedding day completely ruined, either. If anyone could secure an alternate place for a wedding reception, it was Judith Halloway. She had more connections than the circuit board at the Mall of America.

He strode outside and then wished he'd stayed in the library. The courtyard was a mocking reminder of a well-planned schedule completely destroyed.

Cade paused, his gaze moving from the misshapen box-wood, once a family of topiary deer, to the flowering shrubs braided with wild grape vines.

Meghan had confidently declared it would a beautiful place for a wedding. Almost as if she had a clear picture of what the courtyard had looked like years ago. Or what it could be again with some attention.

That kind of vision was a one-way street to disappointment. Cade had decided a long time ago that if he was going to pour his time and energy into a project, he'd make sure he had something to show for it at the end.

Meghan heard the quiet slap of Cade's shoes against the dock and her pulse jumped in time with every step he took toward her.

She hadn't been able to stop thinking about their conversation. Or about him.

There were artists who spent a lifetime trying to achieve what Cade had accomplished at the age of ten. And he'd called it a burden because it didn't fit his qualifications of a "real job."

The look in his eyes when he'd mentioned his mother's friends had peeled back a corner of his soul and exposed an old wound. And made her wonder if ignoring his artistic ability was more a rejection of something Genevieve had held dear than choosing to channel his ability into a more stable career.

Cade stopped several feet away, but Meghan still felt as if she were being reeled in by an invisible tractor beam. Was she about to be fired for insubordination? Or for telling the truth? The glint in Cade's eye wasn't exactly encouraging…

"Are you admiring the fish I caught?"

Meghan exhaled in relief, knowing the proper response would be yes. Too bad she'd never been a fan of the proper response. Something she had a feeling Cade Halloway was used to receiving!

"Fish?" Meghan feigned confusion. "I thought that was the bait you'd been using."

Cade's eyebrow shot up and for some odd reason, it gave her an all's-right-with-the-world feeling. "I suppose you think you could do better."

"No." She bit back a smile. "I *know* I could do better."

"I accept the challenge."

Meghan gulped. "What?"

"I. Accept. The. Challenge. Grab the tackle box."

"Tackle box? Oh, I see. That was your first mistake."

"I know how to fish."

"Keep telling yourself that." In for a penny, in for a pound, as her grandmother used to say.

Cade made a strangled sound that sounded suspiciously like a laugh. But Meghan had never heard him laugh before, so she couldn't say for sure.

"You sound pretty sure of yourself."

Meghan could have argued that point—she'd only gotten good at pretending—but decided she'd stirred things up enough for the day. "Leave the tackle box on the dock and grab the night crawlers. We have about an hour before Bert comes back."

"Anything else?" Cade drawled.

"I get to drive the boat."

Chapter Eight

Fifteen minutes later Meghan decided the fishing competition was rapidly moving its way up the list of Very Bad Ideas. Right past letting the Evensons talk her into perching their cat—she *knew* the Santa hat would make him cranky—on the back of their Saint Bernard for their annual family Christmas card.

How was it she'd forgotten her original plan to put as much distance between her and Cade as possible?

A whopping three feet separated them in the tiny pram. If she moved her knee three inches to the left, it would be touching his.

"Meghan, your bobber."

Was nowhere in sight.

She stifled a squeak.

Concentrate, Meghan.

The line went taut and she grabbed the pole and set the hook.

"Beginner's luck," Cade muttered when she reeled in a nice perch.

"Beginner? I'll have you know that when my family went camping, I always caught the most fish." Meghan felt the sharp pinch of the memory and gave herself a moment to adjust to the pain. As much as it hurt to remember the vacations they'd taken, she'd never wanted to seal Laura's memory in a safe compartment of her heart just to make it easier to handle. "My sisters and I used to have fishing competitions, too. It was the only way Evie and I could get Caitlin in the boat."

"Which one just got married…*bobber.*"

Meghan grabbed her pole again and reeled in another perch, smiling when she heard his soft huff of indignation.

"Evie." Meghan balanced the pole on the side of the boat and carefully took the fish off the hook before depositing it in the bucket. "She's the baby of the family."

"Where do you fit in?"

"Middle child." Meghan's attention drifted to the sun winking through the branches of the towering white pines on the other side of the lake.

It really was beautiful. No wonder the Halloways had fled Minneapolis to spend the summers here. She'd always thought of herself as a city girl, but Blue Key could change her mind. Who needed aromatherapy candles? Not when all she had to do was walk outside and breathe in the sweet scent of the woods that perfumed the air around her.

"Did you take the pictures at your sister's wedding?"

"No, they hired a professional for that." Meghan closed her eyes, feeling the gentle rocking motion of the boat, lulling her into…

"I thought *you* were a professional."

A false sense of security!

Meghan's eyes snapped open and she found herself pinned

in place by Cade's steady gaze. Had he deliberately tried to trip her up or had she stumbled onto dangerous ground by letting her guard down?

"I am…but I was a bridesmaid, too." She held her breath, practically *seeing* the wheels turn in Cade's head as he processed that bit of information.

"I suppose it would have been hard to do both," he finally said.

"Very hard."

They stared at each other for another heartbeat as Meghan sent up a plea for divine intervention.

Cade's bobber disappeared below the surface.

"You have a bite."

Cade's attention immediately shifted, giving Meghan an opportunity to exhale.

Thank you, Lord!

He *still* doubted her credentials. And all it would take was the click of a mouse to locate her Web site and see the screen-size photo of her latest subjects—a herd of adorable miniature horses galloping through a sprinkler—to figure out she didn't exactly fulfill the requirements the Halloway family would have demanded for Parker's wedding.

Meghan's heart took a swan dive toward her toes as reality set in. She'd thought her assignment would be simple. Look for the Ferris. Photograph the wedding. Leave.

She hadn't figured in the amount of stress a wedding created. Or becoming a volunteer gardener. Or being drawn into the mystery as to why the Halloway family had stopped coming to the island.

And she definitely hadn't figured in Cade.

Meghan slanted a look at the man sitting next to her in the boat, threading another night crawler on the hook to replace the one that had just been stolen. The weakening sunlight still had enough power to pick out threads of umber in his dark hair and the intense concentration he applied to the simple task created a slight furrow between his brows.

The sudden flutter of her pulse surprised her even as she rejected the notion. She *wasn't* attracted to Cade. And even if she was, he certainly wouldn't be attracted to her.

It was easy to see that he was the kind of man who'd constructed his life in a precise orderly way, from his career to the methodical way he *fished,* for crying out loud.

Cade was a color-inside-the-lines type of guy. Scribblers drove people like him crazy. She drove her sisters crazy but they loved and accepted her—quirks and all. It was in the fine print of their family code.

Anyone else?

Not worth the risk of rejection.

"Look, Cade! Do you see the eagle? It's sitting at the top of that tree on the point."

Cade hadn't noticed the eagle—but he had noticed Meghan's bobber had disappeared again.

"You have another one. I think your end of the boat is right over a weed bed. I can't believe your luck."

"Luck has nothing to do with it." Meghan summoned a haughty look. "It's skill."

"Skill?" Cade couldn't help but smile. Meghan might have called what she was doing "fishing," but she'd practically created her own sport. He'd never seen anyone so focused on everything except what she was supposed to be focusing on. That she still managed to be successful was nothing short of incredible. "Who did you say taught you to fish?"

"My parents. But I like to put my own spin on things."

"Uh-huh. Would that spin you like to put on things include trying to pierce my ear?" He'd had to duck at least a half dozen times while she recreated some strange contortion with her fishing pole that she insisted was "casting." The last time, the hook had zipped past his earlobe, missing it by an inch.

"That was an accident. And besides that, your ear was in the way."

Cade might have argued the point except that Meghan gathered her hair in her hands and tied it in a loose knot at the nape of her neck. And his brain and his ability to speak parted company.

Once again an image of Amanda materialized in Cade's mind. Amanda kept her hair under control in a short, sleek cut as professional as her navy blazer. If she took up fishing, he had no doubt she'd prefer the smooth, choreographed art of fly-fishing over angling for perch over the side of a rusty, flat-bottomed boat.

He'd met Amanda through mutual friends. They were both independent and devoted to their careers. Shared similar taste in music and movies. They even attended the same church. If Cade had filled out an application for one of those online dating services, he wouldn't have found anyone more suited for him than Amanda Courtland. So why was he content to remain friends?

His head told him that falling in love with Amanda made perfect sense. His heart didn't agree. And right now, it was pounding against his chest wall in response to Meghan's smile.

Which only proved it couldn't be trusted.

"Megs, where are you?" Caitlin demanded.

Meghan held the phone several inches away from her ear,

confident she'd still be able to hear her sister. Caitlin's voice echoed loudly in the predawn quiet of the woods.

"I stopped by a few times but you weren't there. At first I thought maybe you'd decided to stay with Dad another week but when I called him, he said you'd left."

Meghan nibbled on the tip of her ragged fingernail as she picked her way down the path to the narrow peninsula where she'd seen the eagle the evening before.

Maybe calling Caitlin *hadn't* been such a good idea. "I was only in Cooper's Landing for a few days. I'm on a shoot."

"Dad said you were on vacation."

A setup. She'd been right—her older sister and Cade were similar in temperament. "It's kind of…both."

"So tell me about it." It wasn't a request.

"You know, freelance work."

"Where?"

"Wisconsin."

"Could you narrow it down a little?"

"Northern?"

"I thought we stopped playing Twenty Questions when we were twelve."

If Caitlin didn't have such an aversion to sensible shoes, Meghan thought, she would have made a brilliant attorney.

"I'm photographing a wedding."

"You have *got* to be kidding me. I know there are people who think their pets are human, but come on. Who's performing the ceremony, Smokey the Bear?"

Meghan laughed, realizing how much she'd missed hearing her sister's voice. "It's a real wedding, Cait. With real people."

The sudden silence told Meghan she'd managed to achieve the impossible. Momentarily render Caitlin Rae McBride speechless.

"You don't photograph people. And you don't photograph weddings."

"Not usually."

"Not *ever.*"

"Okay, not ever. But I did it as a favor."

"To whom?"

Maybe she hadn't missed Caitlin's voice as much as she thought. "Dad."

Caitlin made a noise that sounded similar to the one Meghan's bicycle tire made when she'd run over a nail. "I can't believe it. Evie was right. I should have known something was up when Dad hemmed and hawed on the phone and wouldn't tell me where you were."

"Evie *wasn't* right. I offered to do it. And it's a small wedding." Meghan assumed it was a small wedding. She'd never asked to see the guest list but how many people could crowd into the little courtyard? Twenty? Thirty?

"Mmm." Caitlin didn't sound convinced.

"You're beginning to sound like Evie. Don't worry so much. I could use some advice, though. Parker wants an outdoor wedding in the courtyard and it's a little—" Meghan searched for the right word. "Unkempt. If I sent you some pictures, could you give me a few ideas how to make it look good?"

"Parker." Caitlin repeated the name. "You don't mean Parker *Halloway.*" A low chuckle trailed behind the last word, as if she knew Meghan couldn't possibly be referring to Parker Halloway.

"She's the bride."

"Parker Halloway."

"Um…yes."

"You're photographing *Parker Halloway's* wedding."

"It's a small ceremony—" Hadn't she said that already?

"Megs, have you met Parker Halloway?" Caitlin interrupted.

"Not exactly, but—"

"Well, I have. She's a princess. Her interior designer is a friend of mine and nothing is good enough for her. Her dad is one of the wealthiest men in the Cities and Judith Halloway, her aunt, is a pit bull in pearls."

"What about her brother?" Meghan ventured. Just because she couldn't help herself.

"Cade? He's brilliant. Great sense of style, though. He likes getting his way. Ruthless—"

Meghan remembered the way Cade had covered Miss Molly up with his coat. And the elusive indentation in his cheek that made an appearance when he loosened up…

"Ruthless seems a little harsh," she said without thinking.

Silence. The second time in less than five minutes she'd had that affect on Caitlin. Then, "How do you know?"

"I…met him."

"Where?"

This time Meghan opted for silence.

"Megs, tell me that Cade Halloway isn't with you."

"Well, he's not *with* me. But he's…here."

"Stay on the line," Caitlin commanded. "I'll be right back."

Meghan delayed her journey long enough to slump against the nearest tree for support. She should have known Caitlin would be familiar with the Halloway family. After all, her sister's business allowed her discreet access to the upper levels of the Twin Cities' social strata.

"I'm back. And I happen to have an excerpt from the Society column that ran in *Twin City Trends* a few weeks ago. Are you ready?"

No, Meghan wanted to say, but she didn't bother because Caitlin would tell her anyway.

"Society weddings of the summer…topping the list of brides to watch is Parker Halloway, daughter of architect and local entrepreneur Douglas Halloway. The themed outdoor reception will take place at the family's summer home and showcase the talents of Chef Michaela Cross of Cape Road Caterers."

Meghan was afraid to ask what "themed reception" meant.

"I'm just the photographer, Cait. Bliss Markham is handling all the wedding details. I'm sure everything is under control." Meghan thought about the courtyard and winced.

From what she was learning about Cade's sister, she couldn't imagine why Parker had chosen the island for her wedding. And suddenly her great idea to pull some weeds and hang luminaries from the trees would be better suited for an impromptu picnic than a reception "showcasing" the talents of a popular caterer.

"She hired Bliss Markham?" Caitlin's voice intruded on her thoughts. "You remember Bliss Markham, don't you?"

"No…" Oh, wait a second. Maybe she did. "She was your first success story, wasn't she?"

"You really do find the silver lining in the storm clouds. I still have nightmares about the woman. I almost closed up shop and took a job folding T-shirts at the Gap because of her."

"But you didn't."

"No, I didn't." Caitlin sounded as if she were pushing the words out between clenched teeth. "She still needs to work on that phony British accent, but she's got a solid reputation as an event planner. I'm not surprised Parker hired her. She's the best."

Funny how two little words like "event planner" could torpedo what remained of Meghan's confidence. A person only needed an event planner when they planned an…event. The small, intimate wedding she'd been imagining fractured into a billion pieces.

"You're wondering why she hired me, aren't you?"

"No." Caitlin responded so swiftly that Meghan believed her. "You're the best photographer I know, but you prefer working with animals. And even though Parker Halloway can be a bit of a cat—"

"Caitlin!"

"—I'm wondering why you took this particular job. The stress around there has got to be off the charts. And where does Dad fit into this?" Caitlin's questions picked up speed. And volume. "And why is Cade Halloway with you? The wedding isn't until next Saturday. You aren't alone together, are you?"

Meghan could almost see Caitlin crossing her arms. And *not* wrinkling her shirt in the process.

"I'd love to talk longer, Cait, but my battery is really low." Meghan tapped the phone against the trunk of the tree. "Oops. I think I'm losing the signal."

"Megs—"

"I'll have to get back to you. But I'll send those pictures of the courtyard soon." Maybe *after* the wedding. "Bye."

The last thing she heard before she snapped the phone shut was Caitlin's squawk of protest.

Lord, what have I gotten myself into?

Meghan closed her eyes; her stomach churning at the thought of the Halloways' A-list descending on Blue Key Island and finding the house and grounds a joke, lacking the country-club atmosphere they'd expected. Lacking *everything* they expected.

Even Cade didn't seem to appreciate that the estate had aged with the dignity and beauty of a vintage postcard. The changing seasons might have stripped some of the color from the paint and dulled the shine on the sculptures in the garden, but to Meghan, those things only added to the island's character.

She detached herself from the tree and stumbled down the trail until it narrowed into a path barely discernable through the thick underbrush, more anxious to reach her destination than she had been when she'd started out.

Bert hadn't made an appearance when Meghan grabbed a banana muffin off a plate on the kitchen table and slipped out of the house to greet the sunrise. She'd only called Caitlin because her sister was awake by five every morning to organize her day.

Meghan had another plan.

Church.

Chapter Nine

Cade wasn't sure what woke him up.

He thought he heard the quiet snap of the screen door off the kitchen and wondered if Bert had gotten up early to work in the studio before breakfast.

He remembered his mother doing the same thing.

Sometimes he'd sneak out of bed and follow her. When he'd peek into the studio, Genevieve would smile as if she'd been expecting him. She'd stop painting long enough to pour milk into a mug and then add some coffee before handing it to him and continuing her work. He still drank his coffee that way....

Cade shook the memory away and silently scrolled through his day, not sure whether he should keep "landscaping" in his schedule or cross it off the list. Once he got in touch with Judith and told her about the state the house was in, he wouldn't be responsible for fixing the temperamental fountain.

The image of Meghan, a smudge of dirt on her cheek as she enthusiastically dispatched weeds from between the path stones, preempted his thoughts like a severe weather broadcast.

And right behind that one came several others, stored like digital photographs on an internal hard drive. Meghan shaking her head and making a "tsking" sound when he'd insisted on using a lure instead of a night crawler—which could explain why he hadn't caught anything. The warmth in her eyes when she'd talked about her sisters. The wry, almost resigned smile that tilted her lips whenever he pointed out that her bobber had disappeared and a fish was halfway across the lake with her worm....

Cade decisively shut down the program featuring "Meghan McBride" and got out of bed.

When he walked past the window, he didn't even have to look outside to know what he'd see. Brushstrokes of scarlet and tangerine painting the sky. Transparent gray patches of mist rising from the lake. The quicksilver flash of a bass surfacing for an early breakfast.

A handful of short summers on the island as a kid and the place had somehow gotten under his skin. He recalled waiting restlessly during the months bracketing his family's trips to Blue Key like a racehorse confined at the starting gate. To make the time go faster, he'd drawn maps during recess of the best fishing spots and filled pages of his science notebook with diagrams of tree forts and rafts.

By the age of ten, Cade had already decided he was going to live on the island when he was a grown-up. Not just for a few weeks out of the summer, either, but year-round. He'd eat fish three times a day and build a canoe so that he could paddle to shore for supplies when he needed them.

All those childish dreams. And in one summer—in one *day*—they'd come crashing down.

Pop psychology claimed that closure was necessary for a person to move on. Cade didn't buy it. He'd been fine until he'd made the decision to visit Blue Key one last time before it sold. He'd thought that coming back as an adult, with an adult perspective, would make the trip easy.

After all, he wasn't ten years old anymore. Over the years he'd accepted his parents' divorce as proof that love wasn't always enough and the whole "opposites attract" school of thought was a myth. Two people had to have similar backgrounds and temperaments to go the distance. He'd even accepted that his mother's unhappiness wasn't his fault.

So why did he stay awake half the night, battling memories from the past?

"Because you're an idiot." Cade answered his own question as he yanked a faded chambray shirt out of the hall closet on his way out the door.

Miss Molly, who'd materialized out of nowhere, barked a cheerful affirmation to his muttered comment.

"Why didn't you go to the studio with Bert?" He glared at the dog as he reached down to scratch the base of her silky ear. "You know I'm not taking you home with me, right? This friendship is only temporary."

She barked again and Cade put a finger to his lips. "Shh. Don't wake up Meghan."

He assumed she was still asleep. He hadn't seen her since supper, when she'd disappeared into the woods with her camera. Much later, at work on his computer in the library, he'd heard her low laughter mingling with Bert's outside the window.

The faint smell of smoke warned him that the two women had decided to make a campfire.

He'd resisted the urge to join them.

It was hard enough to keep Meghan from invading his thoughts without spending more time in her company than absolutely necessary.

"Which way?" He looked down at Miss Molly, who tilted her head, as if considering, before taking several tentative steps toward the lake. Suddenly her nose lifting and she changed course, taking an overgrown path into the woods.

Cade followed.

When the dog's destination became evident, Cade tried to call her back with a whistle. Which she ignored. "Next time I'm putting you on a leash."

Miss Molly glanced over her shoulder, laughed at him and kept going.

Cade's steps slowed as the path through the trees all but disappeared. As he neared the point, he thought about turning around and letting Miss Molly find her own way back to the house but determination—or stubbornness—kept his feet moving forward.

He'd been everywhere else on the island—why not the point? If he was looking for that elusive thing called "closure," he should probably just get it over with. Face the memory head-on instead of trying to avoid it.

A breeze stirred the aspen trees, setting the leaves in motion. Cade smiled humorlessly in response.

Drum roll, please…

He braced himself as he stepped into the open, ready to relive the moment his life had changed. The afternoon he'd searched for his mother and found her. In the arms of a man who wasn't his father.

The image never materialized.

Because another one took its place. And instead of letting his mind rewind to the past, this one held him firmly in the present.

And maybe, if he allowed it, gave him a glimpse into his future.

Meghan. Balanced on the trunk of the old birch tree growing off the end of the point. Eyes closed, face tilted toward the sky. Hands lifted above her head.

She was *praying*.

And if the sight of Meghan's openhearted display of worship hadn't jolted Cade enough, he was struck with something else.

The overwhelming desire to paint her.

And he hadn't painted—or *wanted* to paint—for years.

He took a step back, ready to retreat, but Miss Molly had other ideas. Before Cade could stop her, the dog spotted Meghan balanced precariously on the narrow trunk of the tree and zeroed in on her like a homing device.

Cade opened his mouth to call out a warning, but the words didn't have a chance to form.

Miss Molly bumped against Meghan's leg, the impact enough to shift her balance. Meghan tried to regain her footing, but both of them pitched off the side of the tree into the lake.

And Cade couldn't help it. He laughed.

I will praise you as long as I live, and in your name I will lift up my hands…

Hands still lifted, Meghan laughed softly as one of the verses her "kids" had woven into a mural in the park bubbled to the surface of her silent prayer like a spring.

Until a joyful bark interrupted it.

Meghan opened her eyes and saw a blur of white hurtling toward her.

"Miss Mol—" Meghan pivoted, then gasped as her foot slipped off bark slick with morning dew. As she tried to right herself, the little dog barreled into her and knocked her off balance.

Just before she hit the water, she thought she heard someone laugh.

Meghan bobbed to the surface like a cork several seconds later, but promptly went under again when Miss Molly decided Meghan's head was closer and easier to reach than the shore.

"Miss…" Meghan swallowed a mouthful of lake water as she tried to touch the sandy bottom she knew ought to be below her feet…but wasn't.

"Hold on. There's a drop-off somewhere around here." She recognized the husky growl of Cade's voice somewhere close by.

"I think I found it," Meghan sputtered. She heard a splash as water streamed down her face and blurred her vision. "You were…did you *laugh?*"

"Laugh. Not me." Cade materialized beside her. "Hold still."

Miss Molly stuck her paw in Meghan's eye while Cade tried to untangle the dog from her hair.

"I'll take care of the dog."

"But—"

"Swim back to the tree."

Meghan peeked through her spiky lashes and saw the solid, muscular outline of Cade's shoulder. She reached out and latched on to his arm like a barnacle.

And accidentally dunked him.

He came up coughing and tried unsuccessfully to peel her away. "What are you trying to do?"

"I can't s-swim."

"Then tread water. Everyone can tread water." Cade tried

to disengage her fingers, one at a time, from the death grip she had on his shoulder.

"Is that a proven fact?" Meghan gasped, using both hands to fist the soggy fabric of his shirt during his second attempt to shake her loose. "Because I'm pretty sure I s-sink."

"Just kick your feet and move your arms…"

She could do that.

"You have to let go first."

Meghan wasn't sure she could do *that*.

"Meghan." The warm puff of Cade's breath in her ear instantly multiplied the goose bumps on her arms. "I have a dog on my head and you clinging to my arm. I have to get rid of either you or the rodent. You dec—"

She let go of Cade's arm. From the sound of Miss Molly's ragged panting, the dog wasn't enjoying her impromptu swimming lesson any more than Meghan was.

"I'll be right back. Don't panic."

Easy for him to say, Meghan thought as she made a half-hearted lunge toward the trunk of the birch tree. Her water-logged jeans tugged her down, refusing to let her arms and legs cooperate. She hadn't realized until now that the place she'd chosen to stand, where the birch arched over the water, was at least five feet above the water. And over a drop-off.

"Rule number one. Always swim with a buddy." Cade had returned. He slipped an arm around her waist and pulled her against his side.

Meghan found herself looking right into his eyes. Close enough to see the fascinating merge of color where the cobalt irises deepened to rings of midnight blue.

"I wasn't planning to s-swim."

But hey, if she needed a buddy…

Meghan choked and saw Cade frown.

"Are you all right?"

She nodded mutely, not quite sure how to answer the question. Was she all right? Or did the increase in her heart rate have more to do with Cade than being over her head?

Or, Meghan wondered in panic, were they the same thing...

This was so not good.

She let him tow her toward the shallow water, but as soon as sand sifted between her bare toes, she pulled away. Stumbling up the bank, Meghan collapsed on the first sun-warmed rock she encountered.

Cade dropped down beside her. A little closer than Meghan would have liked, given the unsettling epiphany she'd just had.

"That wasn't exactly on my agenda, but it was an interesting start to the day." Cade scraped his hand through his hair and sent droplets of water raining down.

He had an agenda. Somehow, that didn't surprise her one bit.

"How did you know I was here?"

"You have to give the dog credit for that. She's convinced she's part—"

"Bloodhound." Meghan finished his sentence and smiled. And then it occurred to her that Cade might have seen her *before* she'd fallen in the lake. When she was balanced on the arch of the tree, soaking in the beauty around her, hands lifted in praise.

"How did you know about the drop-off?" Panicked he'd comment on it, Meghan grabbed hold of the first question she could think of.

"That birch tree has been growing off the point since I was a kid. Although it was smaller back then."

"Did you fish here?"

"Not really. My parents insisted on having me in visual range when I took the rowboat out, and you can't see this part of the island from the main dock. I claimed the point as my thinking spot. Parker was too little to make it this far and everyone else thought this side of the island was too wild." Cade's voice sounded detached, as if he were talking about someone else.

Meghan wasn't fooled. The island had to have been a small boy's paradise. For some reason, it became important to Meghan to find a way to reconnect Cade with a place he'd obviously once loved.

"This was the setting for your painting, wasn't it?"

"How did you know that?" Cade's voice tightened.

How had she known? Meghan wasn't sure. Small details had provided clues but it had been more of a feeling than anything. Until now. But the set of Cade's jaw told her that she better have a more logical explanation than intuition. "The curve of the shoreline over there. The aspen trees—"

"I didn't paint the aspens," he interrupted.

Meghan discovered she could raise one eyebrow, too. And it felt pretty good. "The silver-gray splotches in the foreground? Those aren't the aspens?" She dared him to deny it.

He didn't. But he looked away, shielding his eyes. And his emotions. "How did you manage to find your way here? It's not exactly on the main path."

She understood the invisible No Trespassing sign and backed off. What she didn't understand was why he got so touchy about painting.

"I saw the eagle land in the pines last night when we were fishing and I hoped I'd see it again."

"That would have been hard with your eyes closed."

Meghan stifled a groan. He *had* seen her.

"I was praying. But I suppose it might have looked a little…unconventional."

Cade frowned again and it cut straight through to her heart. And put her on the defensive.

"People stand up and cheer when a football player makes a touchdown and no one thinks it's strange," she pointed out. "I think jumping up and telling God wow for a beautiful sunrise is perfectly acceptable."

"Do you always live with such…" He hesitated and Meghan wondered if she should be offended it was taking him so long to find the right adjective. *"Abandon?"*

Abandon, Meghan decided, had a very nice ring to it.

"According to my family, yes," she admitted. "But I prefer to call it *expectation*."

From the expression on Cade's face, it didn't matter what she labeled it. It was still cause for suspicion. She exhaled noisily. "Don't you believe in God?"

Cade swung around to face her and the startled, almost offended, look in his eyes answered the question. "Of course I do."

"What do you believe about Him?" Meghan blurted, even as it dawned on her this probably wasn't the best time, considering they were both shivering and soaked to the skin, to be talking about what Evie liked to call "the meaning of life."

Cade was silent for so long, Meghan thought he was going to ignore her.

"That He's orderly. Everything He created has an intricate design. A reason for being. He has a plan and He sticks to it."

"The master architect?"

"I didn't say that." The color that crept into Cade's cheeks had nothing to do with the warmth of the sun beating down on them.

"What about the rest of the design? The beauty? The color? Trees? Mountains? Rivers? Aren't those parts of the plan, too?"

"Sure." He shrugged the word. "But they're not necessary."

Meghan blinked. "Not necessary?"

"They're…additions. For instance, if I strip a house down to the frame, it still has a form. A structure. But the siding, the roof, even the furniture and the pictures on the walls… those things aren't necessary. On their own, they don't hold anything together."

Meghan floundered in the face of that kind of logic. He was totally missing the point. "If all God cared about was a frame, or a structure, He could have divided the land and sea—in His orderly way—and left it at that. But He added beauty…just for the sake of beauty. He declared all of it *good.* I think those things are important to Him, too. God didn't stick Adam in a cubicle. He put him in a *garden.*"

The words stumbled out and Meghan didn't know if she was making sense or not. She didn't believe the man sitting next to her—the man who had, at the age of ten, managed to recreate ripples on the water with a few dabs of cerulean— thought that if something wasn't practical, it didn't count. That it wasn't necessary.

She tried again. "When you painted the picture of your dad in the boat—"

Cade's expression suddenly iced over, freezing the rest of the words before they left her mouth. "That wasn't my dad. Ferris was a friend of…he was one of the artists who visited the island."

Chapter Ten

Ferris?

Meghan couldn't believe it. Her breath hitched in her chest but she tried to inject a casual tone in her voice. "You painted Joseph Ferris? *He* was the man in the boat?"

Cade looked surprised she recognized the artist's name and belatedly Meghan wondered if she shouldn't have pretended ignorance. But it was too late now.

"Why?" Cade's lips twisted. "Are you a fan of his work?"

"I know a little about art." A slight prevarication, but true. She exhaled slowly before releasing the question she had to ask. "Did he…paint…anything while he was here?"

Cade abruptly rose to his feet. "We should get back and change into dry clothes before Bert wakes up and wonders where we are."

I get it, Meghan thought ruefully. Conversation over. She stood up and rivulets of water poured off her soggy jeans and ran down the rocks.

Miss Molly, who, Meghan noticed with envy, had dried with the speed of an airy white hankie clipped to a clothesline, trotted beside her as she scrambled up the bank to catch up with Cade.

She didn't know why the mention of Joseph Ferris had shut Cade down but the connection between them had been severed. Keeping her distance from Cade Halloway was the wisest thing to do, but disappointment still carved out a hollow in her chest.

And even though everything inside Meghan rose up, waving and shouting, to remind her that Cade wasn't the type of man who needed a friendly hug of encouragement, that's exactly what she wanted to do.

Because he was hurting.

She knew it. She just didn't know why.

Yet.

Your mission, remember? It's to find out what happened to the Ferris, not the Halloway family.

"Don't bother wasting your time in the courtyard today." Cade's voice cut tersely through her thoughts. "Parker is going to have to find another place for the wedding."

"But she won't have time," Meghan protested.

Hadn't they agreed on that the day before? Even though she'd had her own doubts after her conversation with Caitlin, Meghan resisted defeat. But why? Parker's wedding didn't have anything to do with her. In fact, if Cade convinced his sister to move it to another place, it would make life easier. Cade would leave. She would leave…

And you'd never see each other again.

Maybe the pesky little voice in her head had a direct link to her heart but Meghan tried to shoo it away.

"But the cleaning crew is coming tomorrow. And Bliss Markham…"

"Bliss Markham quit."

"What?" Meghan gasped. "Why doesn't anyone want to work for you?"

Cade glanced over his shoulder at her as they reached the main path. "It isn't me they don't want to work for. It's my aunt Judith."

"But Cait—" Caution won out. Meghan didn't want Cade to know she'd been talking to her sister. "I've heard Bliss Markham is the best."

"If Parker hired her, she is."

Meghan tried to keep up with his long-legged stride but she was barefoot and had to keep a wary eye on the roots jutting out of the ground, threatening to send her flat on her face. "If Parker hired Bliss, why would she quit because of your aunt?"

Cade didn't slow down. "You've never met my aunt."

A pit bull in pearls. Meghan had thought Caitlin's description a bit harsh but now she wasn't so sure.

"The cleaning crew isn't a problem. I need them here anyway," Cade continued, still forging ahead as if he couldn't get away from her fast enough. "To get the place in shape for the Realtor's inspection."

Meghan tossed her head toward the sky, appealing for patience.

She waited but it didn't come fast enough.

"I can't believe you're going to sell the island. Parker must have good memories. And she could bring her family here." *So could you.* The thought scraped against a sensitive spot on her heart. The one that spending time with Cade had already softened.

He gave an exasperated snort.

Right back at you, Meghan thought.

"You have so many memories here," she murmured more to herself than to him.

But Cade heard her. Because he stopped dead in his tracks and turned around to face her.

"Selling the estate is a business decision," he said flatly. "And no matter what you might think, not all childhood memories are good ones."

She might have believed him.

If he hadn't added the last part.

Cade's fingers drummed an uneven beat against the top of the desk as he tried to concentrate on some of the work he'd brought with him to Blue Key.

Unfortunately, the image of Meghan—hands lifted to the sky, palms open, offering praise to God even as it looked as if she were waiting to receive something back—kept intruding on his thoughts.

Once again, his fingers itched to hold a paintbrush.

He drummed them against the desk to distract them, but when they idly picked up a pen and started to sketch the curve of the birch tree on the back of an envelope, he surged to his feet.

Meghan hadn't even caught his veiled attempt at sarcasm when he'd asked her if she always lived life with abandon. The question had been based purely on self-preservation. He'd thought it would shut the conversation down. Instead her honest response had pushed it to another level.

Expectation.

That's what she'd called it.

And that's what he didn't understand.

As far as he was concerned, that way of thinking was an open invitation to disappointment. If you didn't expect anything—or more importantly, if you *made* things happen— you didn't end up with…nothing.

Their conversation cycled back through Cade's mind.

He'd never discussed his faith in such an unconventional setting before, but it wouldn't have surprised him to find out *she* had.

Of course he believed in God. He attended the church he'd been raised in faithfully and gave generously when the offering plate went by. He talked to God but tried not to bother Him with what he considered to be insignificant details as he went about his day-to-day routine. His faith fit neatly into his life. It didn't spill over the edges and disturb anything around him.

Why was that a bad thing?

Earlier in the spring, Parker had invited him to church for a special evening series designed to encourage people to "live what they believed" but Cade had declined, assuming he was already doing that. Parker had gone without him and that's when she'd met Justin, a missionary back in the States on something called "furlough" while he waited for his next assignment.

They'd dated for a month before announcing their engagement.

Way too fast, Cade had thought. Less than the expiration date on a gallon of milk.

If he ever decided to pursue a relationship, Cade knew he wouldn't let his heart rule his head. It would be based on mutual interests, not emotions. Conversations would be like a game of chess. Well thought out. Reasonable.

Unlike his last conversation with Meghan.

Talking to Meghan was like playing…verbal Twister.

A reluctant smile tilted the corners of Cade's lips when he remembered his parents having similar "discussions." Never arguments. Discussions. That's what they'd called them. How he and Parker, young as they were, had been able to discern the difference, he wasn't sure.

Maybe it had something to do with the undercurrent of respect in their voices. Or the sparkle of laughter that never left Douglas's eyes, no matter how heated the debate. Or the way Genevieve would catch Cade's wide-eyed stare and wink at him while he listened. An argument would have shut him out, but Genevieve's mischievous wink subtly included him.

"We don't agree on much," Genevieve would tell her children cheerfully when she tucked them into bed, "but we agree on what's important."

Cade had believed her. Until the evidence became too strong not to.

He took a restless lap around the library and a scraping noise outside in the courtyard snagged his attention.

Before he reached the window, he knew what he'd see.

And he was right. Meghan on her knees pulling weeds, her bright hair covered by a floppy hat that shaded her face from view.

Stubborn.

That's what she was.

Why was restoring the courtyard so important to her? She didn't have any connection to the island or to his family. She challenged him. Questioned him. Irritated him.

Inspired him.

Cade turned away from the window but the thought lingered, weighting the air around him.

"Inspires me to what, God?" Cade muttered, directing the question to the only one who could possibly understand. "To do something that wastes my time and energy? I'm maximizing what you gave me, just like the servants in the parable of the talents. Isn't that what we're called to do?"

While Cade waited for an answer, he realized this was the first time he'd talked to God directly from his heart instead of his list.

And somehow, in some way, he knew Meghan was responsible for that, too.

Sheer stubbornness drove Meghan to spend the majority of the afternoon pulling weeds. She discovered that yanking them out released some of her pent-up frustration with Cade. So it was kind of like a two-for-one special.

After dropping the bombshell on her that she didn't need to bother with the courtyard—which she decided to ignore— he'd spent the day holed up in the library and hadn't bothered checking on her and Bert's progress.

They'd just finished pushing a patch of rebellious brown-eyed Susans back to their original borders when a pontoon boat crowded with a lively group of Bert's friends pulled in near the dock. They'd coaxed her on board and encouraged Meghan to come along, but she'd already decided to walk down to the cabins before the cleaning crew descended on them the next morning.

She hoped Genevieve Halloway's habit of displaying artwork in unexpected places meant she'd decorated the walls of the rustic cabins with her friends' paintings, too.

The walk across the width of the island should have given her time to regroup and collect her thoughts, but they remained stubbornly centered on Cade.

He drives me crazy, Lord.

Meghan wanted to say more, but that one complaint kept circling through her mind like the horses on the old carousel as she made her way through the woods.

The four cabins, constructed from peeled logs, hugged the

shoreline a stone's throw from the water. At close range, they looked as flimsy as the card houses Meghan and her sisters used to construct on the living room floor.

A stone chimney sprouted from each blue-shingled roof and all of them had screened porches. Forget-me-nots bloomed around the foundations but the wind had reseeded them in random spots, creating a patchwork quilt of blue and pink everywhere Meghan looked.

Meghan eased the door to the first cabin open and took another step back in time. Hot, stale air that begged for a breeze filled the room. Meghan obliged, rattling the windows until the paint congealed in the crevices loosened so she could force them open.

She gave the interior a quick once-over. No flat-screen television. No television at all. No microwave oven. None of the comforts of the new millennium.

Meghan loved it.

And just as she suspected, a collection of watercolors, oils and charcoal sketches, preserved in mismatched frames, decorated the knotty-pine walls.

Judging from the way Cade had reacted when she'd asked about Joseph Ferris, Meghan had the uneasy feeling that he'd disliked the man. But if that were true, why would he have painted his picture?

She paused to study one of the oil paintings, a portrait of a woman in her late twenties or early thirties. Dressed casually in a red-and-white checkered shirt with a matching scarf tied around her sable hair, Genevieve Halloway's warm smile was reflected in a pair of dreamy, dark blue eyes.

The artist could have interpreted his subject any way he liked, but Meghan had a feeling she was seeing the real Genevieve Halloway. This was the woman who had paid such loving detail to the gardens and carried it into the watercolors she painted. This was the woman who'd proudly framed the flowers her daughter had picked and displayed her son's artwork next to paintings by artists whose work commanded thousands of dollars.

This was the woman Cade no longer wanted in his life.

Remember why you're here, Meghan.

Reluctantly, Meghan moved to the next painting. And the next.

By the time she'd toured the last cabin, the sun was setting and her initial doubts about finding the Ferris had begun to creep in. Anything could have happened to it over the past twenty years and she was running out of places to look.

Bert spent a lot of time in the studio, so other than the time she'd walked Meghan through, there hadn't been an opportunity to check out all the nooks and crannies there.

She stepped out of the cabin and spotted a fishing boat just beyond the point.

And immediately recognized the broad shoulders of the man sitting in it. Cade.

He'd gone without her.

Relief bumped aside Meghan's initial disappointment as she reminded herself she wasn't ready to face him yet.

Farther away, she could see the pontoon boat chugging along the shoreline and hear the faint laughter of the people on board.

The soft tug of loneliness Meghan felt wasn't unfamiliar.

It wasn't that she didn't enjoy being with people. She did. She just chose the people she spent time with very carefully. Evie and Caitlin were her best friends, but she also had a small, close-knit group of people, men and women, she'd known for several years. They were as different as a box of assorted chocolates when it came to ages, hobbies and occupations, but they all had one thing in common—their faith. They valued the things that mattered and they gave Meghan space. Space to grow. To take chances. To make mistakes. To be herself.

And she tried to return the favor.

It suddenly occurred to Meghan that her friends were probably a lot like the people who'd gathered on Blue Key at Genevieve's invitation.

The people Cade had scoffed at.

What did his social calendar look like? Dinner at a trendy restaurant with a private table overlooking the Mississippi? A standing golf date once a week? A black-tie charity event with a woman on his arm who was comfortable in that type of setting?

Even with a little black dress and Caitlin's expert advice, Meghan knew she'd never fit into that crowd.

The low drone of hundreds of mosquitoes emerging from the woods to hunt for their evening supper reminded Meghan it was time to head back to the house.

With Cade and Bert out on the lake, she might have a few minutes to check the upstairs bedrooms. If nothing turned up there, she wasn't sure what to do.

Give up?

It was tempting. By the time Cade got back to the house, she'd be asked—politely—to pack her bags and head back to the city. Cade would have had plenty of time to talk to Parker over the course of the afternoon and his aunt Judith had probably already summoned her minions to find an alternate place for the wedding.

Animals were much less complicated.

Just as Meghan reached the house, she heard the faint strains of music coming from the courtyard. Out of curiosity, she rounded the corner, stunned to see the carousel horses moving slowly, methodically, up and down. As if trying to remember what it was they were supposed to do.

"Hi." Meghan spoke the word softly, not wanting to startle the woman sitting on the back of the white thoroughbred.

The woman didn't bother to look up. "Bliss?" The name was accompanied by a sniffle.

Funny, Meghan had been wondering the same thing. When she'd spotted her, she'd felt a wild surge of hope that maybe the wedding planner had decided not to quit.

"No. Meghan McBride. The photographer." Meghan moved closer.

As the white horse came back into view, Meghan saw the woman more clearly. Close to her own age. Wearing a printed sundress paired with strappy sandals. Sunglasses perched on top of the artfully streaked hair. And even though only one of the colors matched the sable brown of Cade's, Meghan knew she was about to officially meet Parker Halloway.

Another sniffle. "Oh. I'm sorry you wasted your time coming here."

Meghan's first thought was that Parker was crying because she'd seen the shape the courtyard was in. Her reaction would certainly fit with Caitlin's description of Cade's sister.

She watched for an opportunity and grabbed the gold pole of the black charger as it went by, swinging onto the platform of the carousel. "Wasted my time?"

"There isn't going to be a…wedding."

"Because you can't find another place for the reception?"

Meghan gripped the pole tighter as the carousel shuddered and then lurched to a complete stop.

Parker shook her head. "Because I gave Justin back his ring. I can't m-marry him."

Chapter Eleven

Cade came in off the lake shortly after the sun melted into the horizon and took a few minutes to pack away his fishing gear.

He had a nice stringer of fish. The weather had been perfect. The solitude of the lake appealing. But something had been missing.

Meghan.

He should have been happy not to have to dodge her wild casts or compete with her for perch. But instead he'd found himself missing the play of sunlight on her hair and the small frown of concentration that settled between her eyebrows when she baited the hook.

What was she doing to him?

He refused to let his thoughts formulate an answer to that, knowing he was afraid of the answer.

"Come on. Rise and shine." He glanced down at Miss Molly, who'd fallen asleep on a musty boat cushion while he cleaned the fish. "Let's find…" *Meghan?* He quickly ad-libbed. "Something to eat."

The dog's ears perked up at the word "eat" and for once she followed him obediently up the path to the house.

Cade had almost reached the front door when he heard music. Carousel music. He recognized the grating tune immediately.

Only one person could have coaxed the ancient contraption to life. And that one person had to know that some things were off limits.

Shadows already filled the spaces between the flowering bushes and shrubs as Cade veered around the hedge of arbor vitae.

The music stopped abruptly and so did Cade.

Meghan sat on a willow bench near the carousel, one arm curved around the shoulders of the young woman hunched over beside her.

It took a few seconds to realize it was his sister.

"Parker?" Cade walked toward them but Parker met him halfway, launching herself into his arms.

He couldn't remember a time when his sister had been anything but calm, confident and in control. And the last time she'd turned to him for comfort was when she'd fallen off her tricycle and skinned her elbow.

"Hey." Awkwardly, he pushed the damp strands of hair off her face as she burrowed against him. "What's going on?"

He asked the question even though he could guess the answer. Parker had seen the courtyard and now she finally believed what he'd been trying to tell her.

He peeled his sister off his chest, about to give her a gentle shake to remind her to pull it together, but Meghan's fingers closed over his. And squeezed. Hard.

"We should go inside," she murmured.

Cade hesitated and then nodded curtly, guiding Parker up the path to the house while she clung to him like a limpet.

"Who brought you over? Is Justin here?" Cade thought the questions were simple and straightforward enough but all they did was trigger another bout of tears.

Meghan had the door open, waiting for them, before they reached it. He would have led Parker into the library, but Meghan got in his way and somehow the three of them ended up in the kitchen.

Cade assumed Meghan would leave them alone to talk but she set a box of tissue down in front of Parker. "Tea? Coffee?"

Cade opened his mouth to tell her neither one was necessary but closed it again when Parker melted against the chair and let out a long, shuddering breath. "Tea. Please."

Cade didn't know if he should be relieved or frustrated that Meghan had stayed. It was family business, after all, and he'd never seen his sister so rattled. He pulled out the chair opposite Parker and straddled it, folding his arms across the back. Parker honked loudly into a tissue, seemingly unaware of the black streaks of mascara running down her cheeks.

"I tried to warn—" The rattle of teacups interrupted him. When he glanced at Meghan, the message in the misty-green eyes was clear. No *I-told-you-so's allowed.* Maybe she had a point. And he didn't want to be responsible for opening another set of floodgates, either. "Don't be upset, Parker. We can fix this. Have the ceremony at church and let Aunt Judith find another place for the reception. We're got time and everything else is good to go, right?"

In spite of his brotherly pep talk, tears pooled in her eyes again.

To Cade's astonishment, Meghan slipped a cup of tea in front of Parker and put a comforting hand on her shoulder.

What was even more surprising was Parker's reaction. Instead of moving away from Meghan, his sister reached up and grasped her hand as if it were a lifeline.

"I'm not upset because of the courtyard. It's p-perfect." Just as Cade tried to wrap his mind around that, Parker dropped another bomb on him. "Justin and I… I c-called it off. The wedding is off."

"What happened?" Cade tried to mask his relief. He hadn't expected such a neat little solution to all their problems.

Parker shook her head mutely, staring into the teacup, and Cade glanced at Meghan. She looked away, but not before he saw mixture of disbelief and disappointment in her eyes. She'd accurately read his thoughts, another unsettling habit of hers.

Cade tried to tell himself that she, as an outsider, didn't understand the whole situation. How could she know that Parker, whose idea of "roughing it" was skipping her weekly spa appointment, wasn't being realistic about linking her future to a missionary used to going without the most basic necessities? Like clean drinking water. Or outlets to plug in the dizzying array of tools Parker used to style her hair.

Parker's stubborn insistence to plan a wedding in three months, before Justin returned to Mexico, had only added to the family's concern that she was letting her heart rule her head.

But no one had been able talk her out of it. Not even Judith. For some reason Parker was blind to the fact she and Justin were as ill-suited as…their parents.

"It's better this way," Cade said cautiously instead. "One of these days, you'll look back and be glad you called off the wedding. You wouldn't want to find out Justin wasn't the right one for you *after* you got married."

Meghan had heard enough.

She had to leave the room before she muzzled Cade with the nearest dish towel. And she was taking Parker with her.

Before Cade had interrupted them, Parker had started to open up to her about the reason she'd broken up with her fiancé and fled Minneapolis for Blue Key Island.

Her. A complete stranger. Finding things out about Parker that none of her family members seemed to know.

Which wasn't surprising, Meghan thought darkly, if the Halloways considered lectures and interrogations "the art of conversation."

"Cade, I'll bet Parker hasn't had anything to eat all day. Why don't you make her a veggie omelet while I help her unpack." Meghan phrased it as a statement, not a question.

Cade opened his mouth to say something but his jaw snapped shut when Parker offered him a watery smile. "That sounds great."

"Great," Meghan echoed cheerfully.

The suspicious glint in Cade's eyes told her that he knew she was up to something. Her answering smile told him she didn't care.

Parker followed her down the hall like a sleepwalker and Meghan moved to the side as Parker stepped past her, into the pink bedroom she'd slept in as a child.

"It looks exactly the same." Parker's voice came out barely above a murmur as she ran her hand over the sun-bleached taffeta spread.

Meghan didn't hear any bitterness in the other woman's tone, only quiet resignation.

"Those shoes have to be killing your feet," Meghan said, eyeing the railroad-spike heels. "I have some slippers you can borrow. I'll be back in a flash."

She slipped out of the room and her nose twitched at the pungent scent of garlic permeating the hall. Apparently, Cade had taken her advice.

When she returned, Parker was perched on the side of the bed, examining her face in a compact mirror.

"I look horrible." She snapped the mirror shut without bothering to repair the damages.

"You look a little…rumpled." If Meghan would have said anything else, Parker would have known she was lying. "But that's understandable."

She offered her the dog slippers—a gag gift from Caitlin when she'd opened her studio—complete with tails and the curling, pink felt tongues she was forever stepping on.

Parker studied them for a few seconds before pushing the slippers on her feet. She wrapped her arms around her knees like a little girl and looked around. "This room seems a lot smaller than it did when I was six. I love it here."

Love. Present tense, Meghan noticed, not past. And unlike Cade, no bitterness leaked into Parker's voice. How could it be that two people who shared the same memories had such different feelings about the island?

"When J-Justin and I started making plans, I couldn't imagine another place I'd rather say my wedding vows," Parker continued softly. "It just seemed to be the right place for a new…a new beginning."

Meghan silently agreed. She'd fallen in love at first sight, too. Even in the neglected state it was in, the house retained an inviting, comforting warmth. The grounds reflected Genevieve Halloway's attempts to work with the wild, untamed beauty of the island instead of trying to subdue it.

"Now I wonder if there really is such a thing as a new

beginning. If a person can really change." Parker picked at a loose thread in the bedspread, her expression pensive.

Meghan's forehead furrowed. "Were you hoping Justin would change?" she ventured.

Parker looked up, startled. "Why would I want Justin to change? He's the most amazing man I've ever met. Strong. Sensitive. Funny. Caring. Unselfish." Her voice wobbled slightly on the last word. "His faith is…different. It took me a while to figure out it was what made *him* different. He knows God in a way I never thought a person could. In a way that *I* could."

"I understand."

Parker pinned her with a sharp look, then relaxed. "You do, don't you? I can see it in your eyes."

"What I don't understand is why you broke your engagement," Meghan said candidly. "It's obvious you love Justin."

"Love isn't always enough," Parker muttered.

"Do you really believe that? Or is that someone else talking?" *Say, someone a smidge over six feet tall, with cobalt-blue eyes?*

Parker stared at her for a long minute and then her gaze shifted to the rocking chair in the corner. "Why am I talking to you? Who are you? I don't even know why you're here."

Meghan wasn't intimidated by the unexpected glimpse of the Parker Halloway that Caitlin had described. The sudden retreat behind familiar walls had to be a defense mechanism. Something Meghan understood all too well.

"You do know why I'm here. Because God obviously thought you needed someone—" *other than your brother* "—to talk to you about why you're willing to walk away from the man you love."

Parker's response was to bury her face in one of the daisy-shaped pillows piled at the end of the bed and Meghan strained to make out the muffled words underneath them. "I think God is going to give up on me. I keep trying...but I keep messing up."

"What is it you're trying to do?"

Parker sat up, ticking off the list on each manicured finger. "Be friendly. Polite. Generous. Kind. Unselfish—"

"You're trying to be a Girl Scout?"

"I'm trying to be a missionary's wife," Parker blurted. "And I can't do it. Aunt Judith is right. If I really love Justin, I have to accept I'm not the kind of woman he needs by his side. He would end up hating me and I couldn't stand that."

Meghan had to send up a silent prayer, asking God to forgive her bad attitude toward Judith Halloway, before she spoke again. Obviously, Parker's aunt had failed to break up the engagement by telling her niece that Justin wasn't right for her. But she'd succeeded by playing on Parker's doubts that she was right for *him*.

"You accepted Christ into your heart recently, didn't you?"

The smile on Parker's face answered her question even before she affirmed it out loud. "In the spring. Two weeks before I met Justin. But it's harder than I thought it would be." She lowered her voice. "I still like to shop."

She looked so guilty, Meghan choked back a laugh. "I've been a Christian since I was twelve years old, and trust me, there are a lot of areas in my life still under construction. The difference is that now, instead of trying to manage those areas on my own, I let God in so He can deal with them.

"I don't know if anyone shared this verse from Romans with you, Parker, but it says God demonstrated His love for us in that while we were still sinners, Christ died for us.

"He didn't wait until we had our act together before He

decided we were good enough to love. He loved you before you knew Him and He loves you now. And He doesn't expect you to do your own heart makeover, either. That's His job. I've found it's spending time with Him that changes me. It's not something I have to force. If that's the case, it becomes all about me again, when really, it should be about Him."

For the first time, hope sparked in Parker's eyes. But then the doubts returned and she chewed off the last smidge of color remaining on her bottom lip. "I don't know, Meghan. I might drag Justin down. I don't have the books of the Bible memorized and I'm not sure if I'm praying the right way. I don't even know how to make a casserole if the church has a potluck dinner—"

"How old is Justin?" Meghan interrupted.

"Twenty-eight."

"I may be wrong, but Justin has probably met plenty of women who know how to make cheesy potatoes and Jell-O fluff. But he didn't fall in love with one of them and ask her to marry him. He asked you. He loves *you*. If you really believe God brought you and Justin together, don't let your fears get in the way. Or your aunt Judith."

"Aunt Judith." Parker shook her head. "She means well."

Meghan wasn't so sure about that, but was saved from having to comment by a light rap on the door.

"Ladies, dinner is served." Cade bowed low, a white dish towel draped over his arm.

Parker giggled and jumped off the bed.

Cade looked down at her feet as she padded toward him. "Interesting choice of footwear, sis."

"They're Meghan's."

"Really?" Cade smiled, and the tiny crease in his cheek made a guest appearance.

Meghan swallowed hard against the lump that suddenly formed in her throat. Fatigue? Discouragement that she hadn't found the Ferris during her search of the cabins? Or because she'd expected Cade to be all business but he'd somehow known that what Parker really needed was her big brother?

And that small, silly gesture scooped out another piece of her heart. If Cade Halloway kept it up, it wouldn't be long before he had the whole thing.

And that scared her more than anything.

"Aren't you coming, Meghan?" Parker paused, and glanced back.

"I should take Miss Molly for a walk since Bert won't be back until later."

Parker's eyes narrowed and Meghan had the sudden, uncomfortable feeling the other woman could see right through the flimsy excuse. And why she'd made it.

"What time do you get up in the morning?" Parker asked.

"About seven." Curiosity overrode caution. "Why?"

"Because I've only got five days to plan a wedding and I need your help."

Chapter Twelve

Cade watched his sister tuck away three-quarters of the omelet he'd made, plus two pieces of toast. All the time eyeing the slice of ham he'd cooked up for himself.

With a sigh, he slid it onto her plate and received a sunny smile in return. He still couldn't believe the transformation in his sister after ten minutes in Meghan's company. Apparently he wasn't the only Halloway susceptible to her wide-eyed optimism.

"Dad called." Cade reached for the teapot and topped off Parker's cup.

"You didn't tell him I was here, did you?" Panic flared in his sister's eyes.

"He was worried."

"He'll tell Aunt Judith," she predicted gloomily. "And she'll airdrop a team of deprogrammers on Blue Key by tomorrow morning."

"I can always set a trap for them. It worked pretty well the last time I tried it, as I recall."

Parker smiled. "You didn't expect it to, though, did you? I'm glad I still have all my toes."

Cade grinned. "We won't talk about that."

Silence settled between them and the laughter in Parker's eyes faded. "There's a lot we won't talk about, isn't there, Cade?"

He shrugged, knowing what she was referring to and yet reluctant to go down that road. "There's no point in digging up the past. Especially when it comes to Dad and Genevieve. She wanted something else out of life and she left. She left Dad. She left us. End of story."

At least that's all Parker needed to know.

"You never call her Mom," Parker murmured.

"I don't know anything about her. And it's hard to call someone Mom who you haven't talked to in twenty years…" Cade leaned forward, stunned to see tears form in his sister's eyes again. "What?"

She took a deep breath and met his gaze. "I talked to her."

"When?"

Parker flinched and Cade realized he'd put more force in the word than was necessary. He counted to ten. And then to fifteen. His voice softened. "When?"

"In April."

April. The same month she'd met her fiancé. A dozen questions surfaced and Cade swiftly ranked them in order of importance. "Does Dad know?"

"I wanted to tell him."

So, no. Some of the muscles in Cade's neck loosened. He could only imagine the fireworks that confession would have created in the family.

"Why after all these years of silence, did you think Genevieve would want to know—would *care* to know—about Justin?"

Silence stretched between them and Cade realized his little sister was trying to decide if she could trust him. And it stung. Maybe as far as sibling relationships went, they weren't extremely close but he'd always kept a watchful, brotherly eye on her from a distance.

"I didn't call Mom to tell her I met Justin. I called to tell her that I met…Jesus."

It was the last thing he expected her to say. "Parker—"

"I know what you're going to say but just listen to me for a minute, Cade. I have a relationship with God now. And it's different. When we went to church, it was a Sunday-morning appointment. Like getting my nails or hair done. If I paid attention to anything, it was what the other women were wearing. And it's scary how I thought that was normal. That it was *enough.* But something happened when I started going once a week to hear the missionaries talk. It was like listening to a different language that everyone could speak but me. They talked about God as if He wasn't just glaring down at everyone from heaven, but like He was right there with them. And that He loves them. Cares what happens to them. I…I wanted that. And I never knew I wanted it until then.

"I'd been meeting with the pastor's wife, studying the Bible with her. We talked about forgiveness one day and I realized it was crazy that our family split apart so completely, no matter what the reason. That because our parents divorced when I was six years old, I have to live the rest of my life without knowing my mother."

"It's what Genevieve wanted."

"It's not what I want." Parker's voice was soft but emphatic.

* * *

Cade dropped onto the willow bench and closed his eyes, even though darkness cloaked the courtyard and he couldn't see anything more than two feet in front of him.

Bert had returned from her boat ride, thrilled to see Parker again no matter what the circumstances, and he'd turned his sister over to her for a reminiscing marathon, grateful for the chance to escape.

Too bad he couldn't escape his thoughts as easily.

He was still having a hard time processing what Parker had told him. That she'd been in contact with their mother. That Genevieve had hinted she'd like to see Parker sometime if Parker was agreeable. And Parker seemed more than agreeable. She was actually excited about the possibility of, in her words, starting over.

That was another thing Cade didn't get. Starting over. No one could reclaim twenty years. Parker had been in first grade when Genevieve left and now she was an adult. They were more like strangers than family members.

And why was Genevieve suddenly interested in getting to know her daughter?

According to Judith, Genevieve had signed the papers granting total custody of her children to Douglas without protest. And his aunt had hinted the generous settlement their father had given Genevieve had played a significant part in the decision.

They didn't know anything about Genevieve or the kind of life she was living now. Judith had judged Genevieve selfish, but she could also be an opportunist, ready to take advantage of her only daughter's desire to reconcile.

The thought made Cade shifted restlessly and his hand bumped something on the bench beside him. He reached out and picked it up. Meghan's camera. She must have left it here when he'd found her and Parker sitting together earlier.

Cade shook his head. It wasn't the first time he'd seen it lying around, but he couldn't believe she'd left it outside—what if it rained during the night?

"Cade?" Meghan suddenly stepped out of the shadows, as if conjured up by his thoughts. "How is Parker doing?"

"Carrying on with her wedding plans." *Thanks to you.*

Cade didn't say the words out loud but he didn't have to. The unspoken accusation hung in the air between them.

"What do you have against Justin?" Meghan finally ventured.

"I don't have anything against Justin," Cade said, surprised. "I've met him and I think he's a great guy."

"Then why…" Meghan's voice trailed off in confusion.

"They're complete opposites," Cade explained patiently. "Justin is soft-spoken and thoughtful. He's used to making sacrifices. To putting other people first. Parker is used to getting her own way. Very loudly, on occasion. The qualities they're drawn to in each other will eventually drive them crazy." *And drive them apart.*

"Maybe. But they could complement each other, too."

"Like oil and water?" Cade asked cynically.

She tilted her head. "Like hot fudge and ice cream."

"Like my parents?"

The corners of Meghan's lips turned up. "Like mine."

"I think you're overestimating my sister."

"And I think you're underestimating two people who are committed first to Christ and second to each other," she said quietly. "Maybe what they bring to the relationship might be different, but they're building on the same foundation. Their faith."

Cade didn't know what to say. Maybe understanding that

was what had sparked the peaceful glow he'd seen in Parker's eyes after she'd talked to Meghan.

His fingers closed around the camera and he held it out, grateful for the chance to take a detour from the path their conversation was going down.

"You left your camera on the bench," he said abruptly.

Meghan took a tentative step forward to take it and her fingers brushed against his. The slightest touch, but Cade felt the jolt down to his toes.

"Someone should invent one of those beeper things for cameras." Her soft laughter stirred the evening air. "Then I'd always know where it was."

"Or you could put it back in the same place every time you used it." Cade thought the suggestion was a reasonable one, but it snuffed out the sparkle in her eyes like a bucket of water on a campfire.

"I'll keep that in mind."

Cade watched her walk away and disappear into the shadows, feeling like an insensitive clod. The worst part was, he wasn't sure why.

"Did you get the pictures I sent? How do we start?" Meghan surveyed the courtyard, hoping her sister had formulated a plan.

"Mmm. For starters, I'd recommend a backhoe. Definitely a backhoe. And a bulldozer."

"Caitlin!"

"Is Parker Halloway's themed reception a recreation of Gilligan's Island?"

"I need advice, not a stand-up comedy routine."

"Who's joking?"

"Cait—"

"Fine. What time is the ceremony?"

"Three o'clock?"

"Reception?"

"Five." Meghan smiled as Parker sidled closer and she held the phone out a few inches to include her in the conversation.

"Too bad. Darkness would have definitely worked in your favor. But I suppose the times are etched in stone." Caitlin expelled a "look what I have to work with" sigh.

"What's etched in stone?" Parker whispered.

"The ceremony and reception time," Meghan whispered back.

"No, it isn't. What does she have in mind?"

"Parker said it isn't. What do you have in mind?"

Silence. And then, "Are you sure she's really Parker Halloway and not an impost—"

Meghan squeaked and jerked the phone back but it was too late. Parker had heard. "It's really me, Caitlin," she sang out cheerfully.

"I'm never going to work in this town again," Caitlin muttered.

"Yes, you will. Now focus. Wow, it feels good to say that to *you* for a change. Now, one more time. What do we need?"

"Bliss Markham," Caitlin admitted. "But I heard she took a flight to Paris for a long weekend. Something about needing to recuperate?"

Parker rolled her eyes and mouthed the words "Aunt Judith."

"Okay, this is a list of what I need to start with." Caitlin got serious and shifted into image-consultant mode. "Measurements of the courtyard. Number of guests. Menu. Weather forecast for the weekend. Floral arrangements… Megs? Are you still with me? Repeat what I just said."

Meghan winced. "Ah...menu?"

"Maybe you should write this...never mind. Let me talk to Parker."

"Be nice." Meghan whispered the warning before handing the phone to Cade's sister.

Bert came outside, carrying a tray with a pitcher of orange juice, a plate of cinnamon rolls and a carafe of coffee.

"Fuel," the caretaker said succinctly.

Meghan glanced at the door behind Bert, waiting for Cade to make an appearance. If he was still on the island. She'd sensed the change in his mood last night and wondered if he was upset that Parker was going ahead with the wedding plans.

If Caitlin met someone like Justin, Meghan knew she'd be thrilled to welcome him into the family. Evie had been blessed with that kind of man in Sam, and Meghan couldn't have been happier for her younger sister. Their wedding had been a celebration of God bringing two people together in His name.

Her brother-in-law was a new believer, like Parker, but his faith was already bearing fruit. Evie had shared that Sam had started the process to create a chaplain's ride-a-long program through the Summer Harbor Police Department, not only to encourage the officers but to reach out to families in the community.

"Penny for your thoughts." Bert deftly poured a cup of coffee and pressed it into her hands.

Meghan smiled. "I was thinking about my sister's wedding. It was perfect. Not everything-just-so perfect, but perfect in its...imperfections, I guess you could say. We decorated the tables with white linen and crystal but the cen-terpieces were wildflowers in antique glass vases. My dad's friend, Sophie, made the wedding cake. It was important to Evie that all of us contributed something to make the day special. It wasn't an event. We were celebrating how awesome it is when God brings two people together."

"That's what Justin and I want."

Meghan hadn't realized Parker was eavesdropping on their conversation. "But *Twin City Trends* said your wedding was going to be the one to watch," Meghan reminded her.

"That wasn't my dream wedding, it was Aunt Judith's. And it also happened to be the one that got canceled yesterday." The mischievous gleam in Parker's eyes—eyes a shade lighter than Cade's—brightened. "Which means the wedding we're planning now can be anything we want it to be."

Parker put the phone back to her ear. "Caitlin? Are you still with me? Guest list, let's say twenty. Six o'clock ceremony. Eight o'clock reception." She nudged the phone down her chin and looked at Bert. "I no longer have a florist or a caterer, but can you whip up some hors d'oeuvres? And a wedding cake?"

"I'd love to." Bert grinned.

"Great. Caitlin? I'll call you back. Before we go any further, I need to make one more phone call and ask Justin to marry me."

Later that afternoon, sketchbook under her arm, Meghan broke away from the frenetic whirlwind of activity and headed for the point in a quest for peace and quiet…and the opportunity to fall apart without witnesses.

Somehow, Parker had assumed she was as qualified as Bliss Markham to oversee the wedding preparations.

"Maybe it's because she thinks you've photographed so many weddings you have a handle on the way these things are supposed to work," Meghan muttered as she stumbled along the uneven path.

Guilt pinched her for the first time since she'd come to Blue Key Island.

No one can serve two masters…

The scripture reference scrolled through her mind and Meghan shook it away.

Completely out of context, she told herself firmly. Technically, she did have two employers—Parker Halloway and Nina Bonnefield—but she'd thought she could keep the two jobs separate. She didn't realize she'd find herself at cross-purposes. But she didn't know she'd be drafted into service as a stand-in wedding planner, florist and gardener, either! Fortunately, Bert had taken on the role of supervisor for the cleaning crew that arrived just before lunch to shoo the mice out and transform the cabins into acceptable living quarters.

Parker's wedding had been ruthlessly scaled down from a "summer event" to a small, intimate gathering of close friends and family, but Meghan had still spent the afternoon trying to create what Caitlin liked to refer to as a "plan of attack."

But then, General Caitlin thrived on that sort of thing. Three hours later, Meghan was retreating into the brush, ready to surrender.

Except that Parker was counting on her. And explaining why she didn't have a hundred simple wedding solutions right off the top of her head would mean explaining the real reason she'd signed on to photograph the wedding.

Meghan felt another pinch of guilt.

To tell Parker the truth now would not only break the confidentiality agreement she'd made with her father's client but could jeopardize the fragile bonds of friendship between her and Cade's sister.

And it didn't take a degree in rocket science to figure out that Cade wouldn't be happy when he found out she'd been scoping out the island for a valuable painting. A painting its original owner might be planning to "reacquire."

Meghan groaned.

She was in a pickle, no doubt about it. And she had no one to blame but herself.

All afternoon, she'd smiled and nodded. Making and listening to suggestions, pretending everything was under control so Parker wouldn't worry. She'd taken notes but couldn't remember where she'd put them. As she tried to concentrate on one task at a time, old tapes began to play in the background of her thoughts.

You're going to fail. You're going to disappoint people. They're going to think you're strange.

Panic had set in, sending Meghan running for cover. For some time and breathing room to drown out the thoughts with truth.

Lord, the things I'm expected to accomplish over the next few days aren't just out of my comfort zone or things that aren't registered on my spiritual gift list, they're almost… impossible.

Discouraged and tired, Meghan stepped off the path and dropped down on the bank, resting her forehead on her bent knees.

You know the drill, Megs. Evie was an ocean away, but Meghan heard her sister's gentle encouragement as if she were sitting right beside her. Maybe because Evie had told her the same thing a thousand times before. *When you're under attack, pick up the sword of the spirit and parry. Fight lies with the truth.*

Evie might have been the youngest of the McBride sisters but she'd surrendered her life to Christ at an earlier age and many times Meghan felt as if her little sister was the more mature one when it came to spiritual things. And she was also Meghan's biggest cheerleader. Somehow, she understood Meghan's struggles with ADD in a way that Caitlin, who didn't see why Meghan couldn't keep her thoughts focused by sheer determination, didn't always understand.

Meghan closed her eyes, letting her soul absorb the silence as she leaned on the familiar verses that had shored her up during difficult times in the past.

My grace is sufficient for you, for my power is made perfect in weakness.

There'd been a time in her life, like the Apostle Paul, when she'd pleaded with God to take away her weaknesses. To reconnect what she viewed as faulty wiring in her brain. He hadn't. And in the mysterious ways of grace, she'd realized that a one-time miracle of healing hadn't changed her as much as the day-to-day appeals for strength that had deepened her faith.

Quietly, she recited other verses she'd memorized for days like today.

I can do everything through Him who gives me strength.
I am fearfully and wonderfully made…

The last verse snuck in, uninvited, and Meghan sucked in a breath. There it was. The basis of her fears. That people would see the "real" Meghan McBride and find her lacking. People she was beginning to care about.

Meghan sighed. Another visit to a battleground the Lord had already fought—and won—in her life. As much as she tried to move ahead, there were times she returned. The landscape not comfortable but all too familiar.

She opened her eyes just in time to see a bald eagle skim over the surface of the water and then ride the wind current up again.

Meghan choked back a delighted laugh, awed by the unexpected gift. And the reminder.

But those who hope in the Lord will renew their strength. They will soar on wings like eagles; they will run and not grow weary; they will walk and not be faint.

Did planning a wedding, when you had no clue what you were doing, fall under that promise?

Meghan hoped so. Because at the moment she felt more like a fish out of water than an eagle soaring in the sky.

Chapter Thirteen

"So, what do you think?" Parker scratched the tip of her nose with the back of her gardening glove, looking way too pleased with herself.

Which was why Cade didn't have the heart to tell her the truth. "You've made some…progress."

With some strategic planning, he'd managed to avoid getting caught up in wedding preparations for most of the afternoon. Until his sister finally tracked him down and pried him away from the desk, insisting he look at the courtyard.

She wrinkled her nose at him. "We *could* use some more help. But not from the bulldozer that Caitlin McBride recommended."

Cade decided he liked Meghan's older sister. "Maybe the cleaning crew could take an extra day and help out with the landscaping."

"They might. If they didn't already have a month's worth of work condensed into five days. Bert's friends offered to help with the food, but I think we're going to have to bribe some people from Willoughby to come over." She gave him a hopeful look.

"I hate to fog up your rose-colored glasses, Parker, but the people in Willoughby aren't exactly rolling out the red carpet for the Halloway family at the moment."

Parker anchored her hands on her hips; a familiar gesture that made Cade wince. Here it comes, he thought. Level One of what would rapidly morph into the adult equivalent of a temper tantrum. Tools that Parker had used in the past to get her way.

"That's because you're selling the island. It may have been twenty years ago, but a lot of people remember being invited to the island for fish boils and corn roasts. To them, you aren't just selling a piece of property, you're selling a piece of local history."

"It's business. And maybe if the people in Willoughby understood that business requires change, they wouldn't be struggling to keep their little town alive."

He braced himself for Level Two, which could take one of two directions. Shouting or pouting. Personally, he preferred the latter. Much easier on the ears.

Cade blinked in surprise when Parker laughed. *Laughed.* "Can you hear yourself? You sound just like Dad." She walked over and shocked him even more when she reeled him in for an affectionate hug and tweaked his cheek. "Never mind about going into Willoughby to round up some reinforcements tomorrow morning. I'll ask Meghan. I have a feeling she can charm the birds out of the trees. But if she can't get some help and there are still a few weeds on Saturday, we'll have the bridal party stand on them and no one will notice."

She winked and sashayed away while Cade stood rooted to the spot like one of the statues in the sculpture garden.

Who are you and what have you done with my sister?

The question got bumped to the side as Parker's teasing comment replayed in Cade's mind.

You sound just like Dad.

Cade wasn't sure why that statement rubbed him the wrong way. He respected his father. Douglas Halloway had constructed his life in much the same way he'd built his business. In an organized, thoughtful way, controlling—and minimizing—the number of unknown variables. There were fewer surprises that way. Let this in. Shut this out. It worked for them.

He watched Parker kneel down on the cobblestone path and start plucking weeds again, humming a cheerful off-key tune. He couldn't remember ever seeing her so... content. In fact, he'd witnessed emotion meltdowns over things as insignificant as a friend canceling last-minute dinner plans. And although he'd been listening the night before when she'd earnestly described her change of heart, he'd still been skeptical. Until he saw actions to back up her words. Not only would the "old" Parker have demanded nothing less than perfection for her wedding day, she wouldn't have handled the obstacles with a wry sense of humor.

It occurred to him that the change he saw in Parker, the one he'd originally attributed to wanting to put on a good show for her fiancé, might have more to do with a changed relationship with God rather than her relationship with Justin.

Cade wasn't ready for the unexpected stirring in his soul. The uncomfortable realization that his relationship with God looked a lot like his relationship with his own father. Correct but distant. But the truth was, Cade wasn't sure he wanted it to be different. Case in point—Parker. She'd sought a deeper relationship with God and ended up engaged to a missionary. And he still wasn't convinced the match made sense. They didn't have to look any further than their parents for an example of the fallout that occurred when opposites attract.

"Fine," he heard himself say out loud. "I'll go into Willoughby tomorrow and see if I can sweet-talk someone into helping you. I'd hate to have you break a nail."

"Too late. I've sacrificed three already." Parker grinned. "You should take Meghan with you. She isn't such a scowler."

The gleam in Parker's eyes sent warning bells clanging in his head. She didn't think...no, she couldn't think he was interested in Meghan.

"I'm not a scowl—" Okay, he was scowling. But who wouldn't be under the circumstances? "I'll ask her. But only to be the official smiling-person."

Parker shrugged and gave him an innocent look. "Sure. Whatever."

"I think I liked you better before," Cade growled.

Parker's smile turned pensive. "No, you didn't."

"Are you ready?"

Meghan's heart took a swan dive at the sound of Cade's voice behind her. She was going to have to attach a jingle bell to his Rolex, that's all there was to it.

She gave a jerky nod, not sure how to answer his question. Because she still wasn't sure exactly how she'd ended up with Cade as her buddy for a trip to town. It had started out innocently enough. Parker had asked her during dinner the night before if she'd go into Willoughby and inquire at the café about getting a grounds crew together, maybe a few teenagers who'd welcome the chance to earn some extra spending money. It wasn't until after she'd agreed that Parker had blithely informed her Cade was going along, too.

The man she kept trying to avoid. Which was really difficult, given the fact they were on an island.

Nothing seemed to be working in her favor lately.

And did he have to look so good?

Cade hadn't gone native yet—he still favored khaki pants and button-down shirts—but the wind had ruffled his hair out of its conservative style and he hadn't bothered to shave off the five-o'clock shadow that enhanced his jawline. The result was an intriguing combination of business casual and… professional swashbuckler.

Now there was a new style waiting to be discovered, Meghan mused.

"…sent lunch along." Cade hefted an enormous wicker picnic basket into the boat and vaulted in after it. "She must think it's going to take a while to find some help."

Meghan hoped not. She scrambled into the boat and sat down, plucking loose strings out of the frayed hems of her denim cutoffs.

It's for Parker and it's only a few hours, she reminded herself.

Cade must have been thinking the same thing. Because judging from the rate of speed in which he pushed the boat toward shore, he obviously didn't want to spend any more time alone with her than was necessary, either.

"Where to first? The chamber of commerce?" Cade parked his car along the curb in the middle of the main street and turned toward Meghan.

"How about the churches?"

"Churches? Why the churches?"

"Because believers aren't supposed to hold grudges.

Which means that out of all the people in Willoughby, they shouldn't be upset you're selling and they should be willing to help someone in need," Meghan explained.

Cade shook his head at her logic. "How about I go to the chamber of commerce, you go to the churches, and we'll meet back at the park in an hour to see who hired the most people."

"Are you turning this into a contest? Like the night we went fishing?" Meghan asked suspiciously.

"Why not?"

Meghan clicked her tongue. "Men are so competitive."

"Winner gets to drive the boat back."

"You're on."

Cade was late.

So late that Meghan began to wonder if his "divide and conquer" suggestion had really been a plot to ditch her.

At least, Meghan thought in satisfaction, she had the picnic basket.

She pulled her sketchbook out of her bag and began to scribble. Absorbed in the drawing, she didn't see Cade until he dropped down beside her on the blanket she'd spread out under an oak tree.

"You first. How many?"

"Seven," Meghan answered.

"You're kidding me."

"The church youth group at Faith Fellowship needed a community service project." Meghan tried not to sound smug.

"Unbelievable."

"They'll be there tomorrow morning. All we have to do is provide snacks and bottled water and—" Meghan snapped her fingers "—the weeds are history. What did you come up with at the chamber of commerce?"

"You mean, other than a map for a self-guided walking tour of the Willoughby cemetery, which was established in 1864, compliments of Obadiah Willoughby, in case you were wondering—"

"I get to drive the boat, don't I?"

"You get to drive the boat." Cade stretched out his legs in the grass and glanced at the sketchbook in her lap. "What were you drawing? Main Street?"

Meghan closed the sketchbook. But not fast enough.

"Let me see that."

Absolutely not. "I was just…doodling."

"Uh-huh." Cade held out his hand.

"You really don't want to—" She gave in when his eyebrow lifted. Never, she thought, underestimate the power of the eyebrow. "Fine. Here."

Cade flipped through the sketchbook, pausing to linger over some of the pages while Meghan chewed on her fingernail, wishing she could disappear in a puff of humiliation.

"This looks familiar." He frowned down at one of the pages.

Meghan smiled. "It should. You probably drive past it every day. It's the time mural the children's art ministry painted last summer."

"Time mural?"

"You know, there is a time for everything and a season for every activity under heaven? Ecclesiastes?"

"You're involved with Sidewalk Chalk?"

Meghan was surprised, and pleased, that Cade was familiar with the ministry. "More like totally submerged." She didn't bother to mention she was the one who'd spearheaded the entire project. "Have you ever volunteered?"

Meghan would have remembered if she'd seen him on site,

but with the ministry expanding the way it was throughout the various churches in the city, it would have been possible their paths hadn't crossed.

"The firm makes a contribution every year." Cade continued to study the sketch that topped the list of Meghan's favorite murals.

Now Meghan remembered why the Halloway name had sounded so familiar the first time Patrick had mentioned it. She hadn't simply heard the name Cade Halloway because of his family connections, she'd *seen* it. His bold signature had been scrawled in the bottom right-hand corner of several checks giving generous donations to the ministry. There'd even been rumors a black-tie fund-raiser was in the planning stages, compliments of some local corporations.

Meghan didn't pay much attention to the finer workings of that side of the ministry. She was all about the kids and the paint.

"You're the one who comes up with the initial ideas?" he asked.

"I wish I could take the credit. That happens to be one of mine, but there are a lot of gifted people who design the murals. What I do is scribbling compared to some of the artists who donate their time. But I have a flexible schedule, I love kids and I don't mind getting paint in my hair, so it's all good." Meghan scraped up some courage. "If you have time on a weekend, you should help out."

"I told you I don't paint."

Meghan tilted her head. "Do you want to talk about that?"

"No." Cade's lips twitched. Whether from annoyance or amusement, Meghan wasn't sure, but she didn't push the issue.

"Hand out water bottles and peanut butter sandwiches then. If you believe in the ministry enough to support it financially, you should at least see what it is you're supporting. And we need more male role models for the boys—most of the people involved in Sidewalk Chalk are women." The passion and enthusiasm Meghan had for the ministry crept into her voice and Cade shook his head, as if answering another unspoken question. Like, "Where did this woman come from and why am I with her?"

"I'm involved as much as I can be."

Or as much as you let yourself be, Meghan thought.

As much as the ministry relied on donations, she knew four little boys in her group alone who desperately needed someone like Cade in their lives. But what Cade didn't know was that he needed them, too. A lot of the people who worked with Sidewalk Chalk openly shared that although they'd initially come on board with the intent to give something to the children, they'd been the ones on the receiving end of a blessing.

"If you change your mind, all you have to do is show up and we'll put you to work."

"Are you by chance the head of the PR committee?"

"Nope." Meghan reached out to retrieve the sketchbook from his hands but as if he anticipated the movement, he inched away from her and flipped through several more pages.

Meghan tried in vain to distract him. "Should we have lunch before we head back to the island—"

Too late.

"What is *this?*" Cade's eyes narrowed as he tapped a sketch.

Without looking at it, Meghan knew which one he was referring to. The one she'd drawn right before he'd shown up. The one of *him.*

She peeked down at the sketch and saw him pointing accusingly at something.

"A…dimple?" Meghan supposed she should be relieved he'd demanded an answer to a question she actually had an answer for. It was embarrassing enough he'd discovered his likeness in her sketchbook without having to come up with a reasonable explanation as to why it was there.

"A dimple." Cade repeated the word softly. "Why did you give me a…dimple?"

"Because you have one?"

"I do not."

He sounded so offended that Meghan smiled. "Yes, you do."

"I've been looking at this face in the mirror for thirty years. I think I'd know if I had a *dimple*." A slight shudder accompanied the last word.

"That explains it, then. You can only see the dimple when you smile, so I'm not surprised you never noticed it before."

Apparently humor was wasted on him. Cade stared at the page and then touched his cheek in roughly the same spot Meghan had sketched the questionable dimple. He smiled. A wide, celebrity red-carpet smile.

"Is my finger gone?" he demanded. "Did it disappear into the deep crevice you drew on my face?"

Meghan's shoulders twitched as she tried to hold in her laughter. And failed. "I draws it the way I sees it."

As Popeye the Sailor impersonations went, Meghan didn't think it was half bad but Cade didn't look impressed.

"Give me the pencil. It's my turn."

"What? No!" Meghan reached for the sketchbook but he twisted his body away from her, effectively blocking her puny attempt to wrestle it away.

"Payback time. You can unpack the lunch Bert sent. This will only take a few minutes." The glint in Cade's eyes warned her that all her imperfections were about to be magnified by a master.

What had she gotten herself into?

Grumbling, Meghan opened the wicker basket and the yeasty aroma of fresh bread wafted out. Wrapped in a flour towel, the loaf still felt warm to the touch. Bert had added a generous wedge of black pepper cheddar and thin slices of roast beef. White cake with raspberry filling—the prototype for Parker's wedding cake—nestled beside two bottles of iced tea.

Meghan's stomach growled in response to the wonderful sight, momentarily taking her mind off the portrait Cade was drawing. Until she glanced over, instantly mesmerized by the quick, efficient movements of his strong, well-shaped hand.

He wasn't even *looking* at her. But then, she hadn't had to look at him, either. Somehow, over the past few days, her brain had imprinted every one of his features in her mind. And she had the funny feeling they were going to linger there a long time…

Cade had stopped.

It had taken him less than five minutes to sharpen her chin to a point, snub her nose and enlarge her eyes. Meghan sighed. "Let's get this over with. Although in my defense of the caricature I drew of you, I have to say I wasn't being mean. I didn't know you'd never seen the dimp— Ah, the slight crease in your cheek."

"Hmm?" Cade glanced up.

"Never mind. Just hand it over so we can eat lunch. I'm starving."

"I don't know what I—" Cade's jaw snapped shut, severing the rest of the sentence. With one swift movement, he tore the page out of the sketchbook and would have crumpled it up if Meghan hadn't guessed his intent, launched herself across the space between them and yanked it out of his hand.

Chapter Fourteen

"Don't bother sparing my feelings. I deserve…" Her voice trailed off as she stared down at the caricature. "I don't look like this."

Cade frowned. "Yes, you do."

"But caricatures are supposed to exaggerate a person's features. My head should be shaped like a…like a snowcone. And you made my nose *cute*. Not snubby."

"Give it back. I'll do it over."

"No." Meghan smoothed the wrinkles out of the sketch and held on to it protectively. "I love it. Thank you for sparing my fragile self-esteem."

Cade frowned. "What do you mean by that?"

"I've looked at this face in the mirror for approximately twenty-six years," she said, repeating a variation of the comment he'd made earlier in the conversation. "I know my eyes are too big. My hair looks like I stuck my finger in a light socket. My mouth is too wide…."

Cade's gaze suddenly shifted to her lips and Meghan had

to work hard to draw in her next breath. Every fiber in her body tingled as he leaned closer and his thumb and index finger captured one of the long, corkscrew curls that had fallen free of her baseball cap and traced it to her shoulder.

"I draws it like I sees it," he murmured.

Their faces were only inches apart and Meghan was sure Cade could hear her heart beating. She stared into his eyes and wondered if the blend of confusion and hope she saw there was a reflection of her own emotions.

"Meg—" Her name came out in a husky growl and Meghan closed her eyes, anticipating the touch of his lips against hers.

"Cade?"

The feminine voice, saturated with disapproval, separated them as efficiently as a bucket of cold water.

Cade recovered more quickly than Meghan, his expression inscrutable as he stood up to greet the couple. Unlike Meghan, who sat cross-legged on the picnic blanket as if she'd been fused to it, he didn't look at all surprised to see them.

"Hello, Dad. Aunt Judith."

Judith Halloway's winter-blue gaze settled on Meghan. Judging from the woman's frosty expression, it was clear she'd made her own assumption as to what she and Douglas had interrupted.

"Dad, what happened to your arm?" Cade zeroed in on the aristocratic-looking older man, whose arm was encased in a cast from wrist to elbow and supported by a sling.

"It's nothing," Douglas said gruffly. "Just a little mishap."

"A little mishap." Judith scoffed at the description. "A gross error in judgment if you ask me. He decided to go rock climbing over the weekend."

"Rock climbing?" Cade's neutral expression slipped a little, revealing his disbelief.

"I thought I'd give it a try."

"So, what did you think? Mishap aside?"

"I'll probably stick to golf."

The deep undercurrents flowing between the two men rivaled those of the mighty Mississippi and Meghan's eyes bounced from father to son.

Douglas was an attractive, older version of Cade. Silver tipped his coffee-brown hair and he'd passed along the strong, angled jaw and aristocratic nose, but somewhere along the way, life had chiseled Douglas Halloway's lips into a hard, uncompromising line.

That's why the humor in his eyes was so unexpected.

"Now, enough about me. Aren't you going to introduce us to your friend?"

Cade recognized his cue and tried to organize his thoughts long enough to perform the necessary introductions.

"Dad, Aunt Judith, this is Meghan McBride..." *The woman I would have kissed if you hadn't interrupted us.*

His thoughts disintegrated again, leaving an awkward silence as everyone waited for him to finish.

"The wedding photographer," Meghan supplied helpfully. "It's nice to finally meet you both. I've heard so much about you."

Cade glanced sharply at her and the sunny smile she directed his way only managed to bring his attention back to her lips...

He cleared his throat. "What are you doing here, Dad?"

The question might have been directed at his father, but it was Judith who answered.

"We've come to get Parker and take her home, of course." Over the years his aunt had perfected a haughty sniff for occasions just like this one. "I'm not sure why she chose to come here of all places, but she sounded very distraught about canceling the wedding. She'll get over it, but your father and I are worried about her."

Cade and Meghan exchanged looks.

This is your family, a pair of mist-in-the-pines eyes reminded him.

Like he needed to be reminded.

"I was going to call you today—" Cade paused, not sure how to tell them the wedding was back on. And, from the plans he'd heard over the dinner table the evening before, it bore no resemblance to its original form.

In fact, Cade wasn't even sure if Aunt Judith and Douglas's names were still on the guest list.

"Cade was going to ask you both to come to Blue Key," Meghan interjected. "Especially you, Judith. You're right. We really need your help."

Judith drew herself up and pressed a hand against her silk blouse, fingering the triple strand of pearls nestled between the sharp points of the collar. "Of course I'll help. Parker is my only niece."

"I'm glad to hear you say that. Because Parker and Justin are getting married Saturday evening and we need all hands on deck, so to speak."

Cade would have chosen a more subtle approach but when his aunt appeared speechless, he changed his mind and silently applauded Meghan's strategy.

"She changed her mind?" Douglas asked mildly.

Cade nodded, keeping a wary eye trained on his aunt for signs of escalating blood pressure and the other on his father, who didn't look as upset as he should have given the circumstances.

"Parker is very excited." Meghan's engaging smile, like a thousand-watt bulb during a blackout, conveyed the message that they should be excited, too.

"Excuse me." Judith's voice was sharp enough to etch glass. "What did you say your name was?"

"Meghan McBride."

"McBride." Judith's eyes narrowed as she opened the social register stored in her memory file and searched the "M's."

It triggered a protective streak inside Cade that he hadn't known existed. Just as he was about to step in and deflect Judith's verbal missiles, Meghan's eyes flashed a brief warning.

Sit tight on your white horse and let me handle the dragon.

"We've never met. No pedigree, I'm afraid." Meghan managed to sound relieved rather than sorry and Douglas's bark of laughter—quickly suppressed—told Cade that another Halloway had just fallen captive to her winsome charm. "You'll need a ride out to the island and since Cade and I happen to have a boat, you're welcome to come with us."

"Well." Judith stared at her.

Meghan met her gaze, waiting her out.

"Douglas? Shall we? The sooner we get to the island, the sooner I can save Parker from making a huge mistake." Judith smiled as if the idea had been hers to begin with.

Meghan didn't answer. She turned away and began to collect the sketchbook, picnic basket and blanket.

Cade bent down to help her. That's when he noticed her hands were shaking.

"Oreos?" he whispered.

"Double stuff. And I still get to drive the boat."

Cade had to fight the sudden urge to pull Meghan against

him—right in front of his father and his aunt—and finish what they'd started. The only thing that stopped him wasn't the uncertainty of where it would end, but the unsettling feeling he wouldn't want it to.

Smile. Nod. Smile. Nod.

Meghan tried to concentrate on Parker's enthusiastic plans for the bridesmaid's bouquet but her thoughts kept returning to the point. Where the lap of the waves against the sand soothed like a lullaby and the eagle made his three o'clock appearance every afternoon like clockwork. It was as if God had lovingly provided a visible reminder that when she put her trust in Him, she'd have the strength she needed to make it through the next few days.

And Meghan needed strength.

"I'm boring you, aren't I?" Parker laughed. "I know we talked about this last night, but I wasn't sure about adding the forget-me-nots."

"You aren't boring me. I was just thinking." Meghan reached out and squeezed Parker's hand.

Given their different temperaments and backgrounds, the comfortable friendship that had sprung up between them had come as a surprise.

Their shared faith alone provided a strong foundation for friendship, but Meghan knew it was more than that. She truly *liked* Parker. As they worked together, Meghan had discovered Parker was a woman of depth and keen insights. For all her concerns about being shallow and useless, Cade's sister had an empathetic nature and the ability to listen without casting judgment. Qualities Meghan knew would be more important on the mission field than the ability to put together a casserole.

"I don't know what I'd do without you." Parker gave a gusty sigh. "Or Bert…and Dad."

Meghan didn't miss the note of wonder in Parker's voice and knew the reason. They'd expected Douglas to side with Judith about the change in plans, but over the past two days he'd proven himself indispensable…and supportive of the upcoming wedding.

"He manages pretty well with one arm."

"Rock climbing. Can you believe it?" Parker rolled her eyes. "He and Bert are finally talking."

Meghan had noticed that, too. When Douglas had arrived on the island, the tension between him and Bert had been as thick as evening fog. It had taken some time, but the two were now able to carry on a polite conversation. And the evening before, Meghan had spotted Bert carrying a tray of coffee out to the courtyard where Douglas had been puttering with the fountain.

Definitely progress, Meghan silently agreed.

Parker's aunt was a different story. If Meghan had her way, Judith Halloway would be the first person voted off the island. She had to recite every scripture that she'd ever memorized dealing with patience, taming the tongue and loving your neighbor just to be civil to the woman.

After a rocky confrontation with Parker soon after she'd stepped off the dock, Judith seemed resigned to the fact that her niece was going to marry a missionary on Saturday. Too resigned, in Meghan's opinion. She had a hunch the woman was plotting a final showdown and hoped it wouldn't be on the day of the wedding.

"I'm going to check on Dad and see if he needs anything." Parker stood up and stretched, unfolding her runway figure with the grace of a ballerina. "Maybe I'll try to pry Cade away from his desk. He's made himself pretty scarce over the past few days."

Out of the corner of her eye, Meghan caught Parker's speculative glance. And blushed.

"I'm sure he's been busy getting everything ready for the appraisal," Meghan said casually.

Or else he was avoiding her the way she'd been avoiding him.

As forgetful as Meghan could be, the memory of her afternoon with Cade remained stubbornly embedded in her thoughts, surfacing at random times during the day and playing havoc with her already frayed emotions.

"The sale." The sparkle in Parker's eyes faded. "He's determined to go through with it. I think even Dad might be having second thoughts. It's just that Blue Key…"

"Has so many memories?" Meghan gently prompted when Parker's voice trailed off.

"Not only that. It has so much of Mom. This place is the only connection I have with her. It's silly, but when Cade told me he was planning to put it up for sale, I got the strangest feeling. Like if the island was gone…she'd be gone. It was the connecting point for our family. No matter how busy Dad was and how many hours he put in during the year, we were a family here."

Cade might have hardened his heart against their mother, but judging from the wistful note Meghan heard in Parker's voice, she didn't share her brother's feelings.

"Does Cade have the final say as to whether the island goes up for sale?"

"I guess so. Dad shocked us all a few months ago when he revealed his five-year plan. He wants to retire at sixty, about a hundred years earlier than what we all expected.

Aunt Judith thinks he's having some kind of midlife crisis. Anyway, Dad gave Cade the green light to start making decisions, and selling Blue Key was one of them. When I found out, that's when I realized I wanted to get married here. Mom might not be here, but it would *feel* like she was." Parker shook her head. "Justin reminds me to keep praying about the situation but I get confused. How do we know if God wants us to *do* something or if we're supposed to wait?"

Meghan was glad Parker didn't seem to expect an answer. Because at the moment she was wondering if Cade had a five-year-plan, too. And what it included. Running the family business? Writing checks to worthwhile charities? Looking for a woman who looked up to Judith as a role model?

For some reason, it was a depressing thought.

Because the more she spent time with Cade, the more she sensed that he kept parts of his heart under lockdown. Not dealing with things seemed to be his way of dealing with them.

She'd tried that and it hadn't worked.

Eventually Meghan had discovered that giving God room to move through her life meant letting Him clean out the clutter. Sometimes all her soul needed was a daily dusting, other times, a complete renovation…not always painless but much more freeing.

"Oops. Quarter to three." Parker tapped the face of her Tiffany watch. "Time for you to go."

"Go?" Meghan played dumb.

Parker gave her a knowing look. "You know. To the place you disappear to every day around this time."

"Checking out photo ops?" Meghan offered weakly.

"I might believe that. If you took Miss Molly along."

Meghan choked. "How long have you known?"

"A while." Parker shrugged. "I checked out your Web site after Bliss told me your name."

"And you didn't care?"

Parker's eyes sparkled with mischief. "To tell you the truth, the wedding was turning into such a circus, I figured you'd be perfect for the job."

"Does…anyone else…know?" Meghan sucked in a breath and held it.

Parker wasn't fooled by the carefully worded question. "Not from me. You're a photographer, right? And from what I could see, a good one. That's all that matters."

Meghan knew she didn't deserve such loyalty. Especially when she'd come to the island for another purpose. She'd already decided to take one more walk through the studio to see if the Ferris was there. If it wasn't, she planned to hand in her junior spy manual and give up the search.

"I'm sorry—"

Parker held up her hand in a gesture that reminded Meghan of a crossing guard. "Don't you dare apologize. For accepting the job or for taking a break in the afternoon. My family would make most people run for cover." She smiled wryly. "It must have something to do with our charming personalities."

Charming.

And there was the rub, Meghan thought.

It was easier to keep her distance from Cade when he was in alpha executive mode. Much more difficult when he teased her. Or made a detour to the grocery store to buy her favorite cookies. Or told her that she was beautiful…not with words but with a charcoal pencil.

"Off with you." Parker gave her a gentle push in the direction of the path that led into the woods. "Your secret is safe with me. Go let out a primal scream, throw rocks, pray or whatever it is you do. I'll hold down the fort. No one will even notice you're gone."

Chapter Fifteen

Meghan was gone. Again.

Over the past few days, Cade had noticed a pattern emerging.

Meghan spent her time alternating between supervising the teenagers that came across to the island in a ragtag armada of borrowed fishing boats and putting out the fires that inevitably started between his aunt Judith and…everyone.

He'd been stunned and proud of the way his sister had respectfully but confidently stood up to Judith. She'd told their aunt that she was going to marry Justin and if she didn't have her blessing, Parker would understand if Judith chose not to stay on the island to witness their vows.

Judith stayed. And Meghan, through some kind of unspoken vote, had been appointed as Judith's official handler. No amount of icy looks, pursed lips or cutting remarks managed to cast a shadow on Meghan's sunny disposition.

Throughout the day, Meghan taste tested Bert's hors d'oeuvres, answered dozens of questions and sat at the

kitchen table, painstakingly creating luminaries made from
old canning jars and pieces of stained glass threaded on
copper wire.

She'd even put his father to work.

Douglas had been given the dubious honor of taking a pair
of hedge clippers to the overgrown topiaries to decide if the
family of whitetail deer trapped inside the branches was
worth saving.

And then in the afternoons, Meghan disappeared.

Cade wondered about it, but didn't seek her out. Since
their almost-kiss in the park on Monday, it was as if they'd
made an unspoken pact to keep their distance.

For him, it was purely self-preservation. It was bad enough
that the sound of her laughter through the open windows
could totally short-circuit his concentration. Or that whenever
he caught a glimpse of her, his soul reacted like an oxygen-
deprived diver taking in a draught of fresh air.

"Wow. What's the occasion?" Parker's teasing voice
intruded on his thoughts.

"Occasion?"

"You came out of your lair."

"Funny."

"I try." Parker grabbed his hand and skirted a mound of
fresh dirt, towing him along behind her. When Cade saw her
destination was the carousel, he balked.

"It'll break."

"Sit down." Parker perched on the edge of platform and
patted the space beside her. "It's proven it can withstand the
test of time."

Cade sat.

"Were you looking for someone in particular?" Parker
slanted a look at him.

"I needed some fresh air."

"Justin will be here tomorrow." Parker closed her eyes with a blissful smile.

"Stop. I'm getting a sugar headache."

She jabbed her elbow playfully into his ribs. "You should be glad to see him. He's bringing your tuxedo. Oh, and Suzanne, my bridesmaid."

Cade looked at her sharply. He hadn't been tuned in to all the wedding preparations, but he was pretty sure Parker had, at one point, mentioned four attendants *and* a maid of honor. "What happened to Kirsten?" he asked, referring to the woman who'd been Parker's best friend and sorority sister in college.

"She got a better offer. Venice. Paris. She was kind of vague. It's all right, considering the guest list has shrunk a bit now that only close family and friends will be here."

"Mmm. So the guest list would be…"

"Fourteen."

"From?"

"Four hundred and thirty-two."

Cade gave a low whistle.

"I know. More cake for each of us. And cleanup should be a breeze."

"Parker—"

She cut him off with a quick shake of her head. "You remember the old saying that you find out who your real friends are when things get rough? Well, I'm revising it. You find out *if* you have any friends when things get rough."

Cade exhaled slowly. "I'm sorry."

"Don't be." Parker shrugged. "I don't blame people for wondering if frequent credit card use finally melted my brain cells. I love Justin. And I like me better now. For the first time in my life, I feel excited about the future even though I have no idea what's going to happen."

"You've never been impulsive."

"I'm still not." Parker looked at him in astonishment. "Is that what you think? That surrendering my life to Christ and accepting Justin's proposal were decisions I made on a whim? They weren't. I thought—and prayed—long and hard about them. I knew there'd be fallout from my friends and… family. I know what I'll be giving up. For a little while, I admit I panicked and ran away. But Meghan reminded me that if I believe God brought me and Justin together—which I do—I can't let my fears get in the way of our future."

Cade wasn't surprised to learn that Meghan "Miss Expectation" McBride had played a role in Parker's decision to proceed with the wedding.

"I know you have doubts," Parker continued quietly. "You remember how different Mom and Dad were, and you think their differences eventually drove them apart. When we talked on the phone, Mom said she didn't want to get into the details, but I got the feeling there was more to their breakup than what the courts like to call irreconcilable differences."

"She didn't want to get into the details," Cade repeated. "So Genevieve conveniently forgot to mention the affair she had with Joseph Ferris?"

Cade instantly regretted the words when he saw the color ebb out of Parker's face. But it was too late to take them back. And maybe time his sister knew the truth. Maybe knowing would put an end to her desire to "start over" with the woman who'd walked out on them without a backward glance.

"I don't believe you." Parker squeezed her eyes shut, as if blocking him out would block out the words he'd just spoken. "Did Aunt Judith tell you that? You know she never approved of Mom."

He'd opened the door to the conversation, so now he had no choice but to follow through.

"The summer right before they separated, Dad couldn't come with us to Blue Key, remember? He'd been working overtime on a project, so Mom brought us. When we got here, Ferris was staying in one of the cabins. You know how people came and went all the time. He told Mom he'd leave, but she encouraged him to stay for a few weeks to finish the painting he'd started."

He could tell by the expression on Parker's face that she remembered Ferris. A shadow of a memory, because she'd only been six at the time, but it was there.

Cade wished his memories were as vague.

He hadn't let Ferris invade his thoughts in years. Not until he'd caught Meghan holding the watercolor he'd painted of the man.

Bitterness rose up inside him like bile. For a few short weeks that summer he'd idolized the artist. They'd explored the island together. Fished together. Ferris was the one who'd encouraged him to start painting, told him that he had a "gift."

In Cade's mind, his mother wasn't the only one who'd betrayed Douglas. He had, too. Not only because he'd be-friended Ferris, but because he'd actually thought about following in the man's footsteps.

"Mom wouldn't have done that." Parker's voice shook. "She *loved* Dad."

"Genevieve and Ferris had a lot in common," Cade went on carefully. "They both painted. They had the same friends. Enjoyed the same things—"

Parker's chin lifted. "That doesn't mean anything."

She was going to make him say it.

"I saw them together."

"You're making this up and I don't want to hear it." Parker surged to her feet and sprinted across the courtyard, startling the teenagers who'd gathered near the fountain for an ice-cream break.

Cade winced when the screen door slammed shut behind Parker as she fled into the house.

You handled that well.

Scrubbing a hand across his jaw, Cade debated whether he should follow her but decided to give his sister some time alone to sort through things first.

He hadn't meant to be so blunt, but the fact that Genevieve wasn't willing to take responsibility for their parents' failed marriage had stirred up his emotions and temporarily over-rode his ability to think before he spoke.

For years he'd kept what he'd seen a secret, although it was obvious that Douglas had found out. He remembered hearing his parents arguing behind closed doors when they'd returned to Minneapolis and it had sounded much different from the teasing banter he was used to. A week of cold silence from his father—and the sound of his mother crying behind her bedroom door—followed. Until the day he came home from school and found Judith in the kitchen, lecturing a middle-aged woman in a crisp white apron about her "duties."

And Genevieve was gone. Just like that. By the end of the weekend, Judith had replaced his mother with a cook, a day maid and her own watchful, but cheerless, presence in the house.

Douglas retreated into his career. The firm became his sanctuary and he used its walls to close out the parts of life he wasn't comfortable with. He let Judith decide how to deal with the fallout at home from his failed marriage. Cade guessed his father had told Judith not to mention the affair, because although his aunt had been openly scathing of Genevieve's decision to leave in what she tactfully referred to as "a pursuit of other things," she never mentioned another man. And Cade had never told them what he'd seen that day—but age and experience had gradually filled in the pieces of the puzzle until he had a clear picture of what had really led to his mother's abrupt departure from their family.

It didn't matter to Cade that his father had chosen not to confide in him. In his mind, Genevieve's affair with Ferris had simply been a by-product of her unhappiness. They'd tried to make the marriage work, but in the end, Genevieve had turned to a man whose lifestyle meshed with her own. And she'd walked away from twelve years of marriage and two children as if they'd been nothing but a burden she'd grown tired of bearing.

Cade glanced at the house again and felt the gut-wrenching guilt of being the one who'd told Parker the truth.

Chalk it up to an entire week that had refused to go according to plan.

Restlessly, he scanned the courtyard. Aware of the teenagers' curious looks, Cade felt the sudden urge to escape. He chose the closest path that disappeared into the woods and followed it.

There was only one place he knew of that could offer any kind of peace. And he was halfway there when the truth crashed into him with the force of a wrecking ball. It wasn't the solitude of the point he needed.

It was Meghan.

* * *

Meghan heard Cade before she saw him. And when she saw him, she knew right away something was wrong. The rigid set of his jaw warned her that he wasn't going to talk about it.

Tension radiated from him like a force field as he dropped down on the bank beside her and his fingers immediately began to tap out a code against his knees.

She spent the next few minutes trying unsuccessfully to decipher it.

Had he known she was there? Or should she leave?

Cade had claimed the point as his thinking spot years ago, but she'd taken up squatter's rights, figuring the hours he spent in the library meant he'd replaced it as his refuge.

It had certainly become hers.

On the point, the voices and the hum of constant activity were lost in the lap of the waves against the shoreline and the rustle of the aspen leaves.

She stayed there until her heart stopped racing and her thoughts came together once again in a steady, manageable formation. She poured her heart out to God until she could smile at Judith Halloway and mean it.

Cade had been right. No one wanted to push through the dense undergrowth that separated the peninsula from the well-traveled paths.

Except one person, Meghan silently amended. The strangest part was discovering she didn't mind sharing it.

With him.

Ordinarily, her stomach would have coiled into one gigantic knot at having her solitude disrupted without warning. But there was something warm and solid about Cade's presence. Something unexpectedly comforting in the scent of his cologne in the air.

That alone would have sent her fleeing into the woods if it hadn't been for one thing.

The eagle appeared. Right on schedule. And she never turned down a gift. Or hesitated to share one.

"Cade. Look up."

He did. Just in time to watch the eagle take a leisurely lap above their heads before its wing tips curled and it angled lower, skimming the surface of the water. Close enough for them to see the helmet of snow-white feathers and the intimidating curve of its beak.

As if it knew it was playing for an audience, the bird collided with the water and surfaced almost immediately. The fish gripped in its talons flashed silver, like a mirror in the sun, as the eagle returned to the nest.

For a few minutes neither of them spoke. Cade's gaze remained fixed on the top branches of the white pine that cradled its nest.

His expression was remote and his fingers had started their measured tapping again. He obviously wanted to be alone.

Reluctantly, Meghan rose to her feet and took three steps before Cade's voice stopped her in her tracks.

"I told Parker something she didn't want to hear."

Meghan backtracked and sat down beside him again. She might have been tempted to push him into the lake, but heard the self-recrimination in his voice and sighed instead.

Poor Parker. Meghan had been trying to draw Judith's fire away from the bride-to-be for the past few days and now apparently she'd been submarined by her own brother. "Cade, you have to accept there is going to be a wedding here the day after tomorrow—"

"It wasn't about the wedding," Cade interrupted. "It was about Genevieve."

Meghan sucked in a breath and waited. Cade always referred to his mother by her first name and she guessed it was his way of detaching himself from the bond they shared as parent and child.

"Parker just couldn't leave well enough alone. And she has no idea what Dad will do if he finds out she contacted Genevieve," Cade muttered. "My sister doesn't usually do things like this, but lately it's been one crazy decision after another. She's listening to her heart, not her head."

"Or maybe they're working together."

The impatient look Cade shot in her direction disagreed. "After all this time, Parker is willing to let Genevieve waltz back into her life. As if the woman went to the mall and happened to be gone for, oh, twenty years. Can you believe it?"

"Yes," Meghan said simply, astounding them both. "Parker is at a new place in her life. She's ready to forgive and move on. She's getting married…she and Justin might have a family of their own. It's all right if she wants to make some extra room for people she cares about."

She had never been in a situation like the Halloways', but she did know that holding on to bitterness and anger took up a lot of room inside a person and crowded out the fruit that God tried to cultivate in His children.

"Parker doesn't know anything about her," Cade said flatly. "She thought Genevieve left because she didn't want to be tied down by a family. I told her the truth to save her from getting hurt again."

Meghan swallowed hard and sent up a silent prayer for strength. Not only for herself, but enough to share with Cade. It was clear from the expression on his face that he was hurting, too. "What did you tell her?"

"That Genevieve had an affair with Joseph Ferris."

Meghan thought she'd braced herself for whatever his response would be, but the impact still sent shock waves through her.

"But—"

"I saw them together." Cade designed his words to shut down any opposing arguments. "Right here as a matter of fact. Dad had shown up a few days early to surprise us and he sent me to find her. I looked everywhere—the point was the last place I tried. They didn't hear me but I saw them. Saw their arms around each other. I didn't understand what was going on at the time, but something didn't seem right."

Meghan couldn't imagine the confusion a ten-year-old boy would feel in that situation but denial struggled alongside compassion for Cade. Call her misguided, but something inside her refused to believe that Genevieve Halloway would willingly sacrifice her family for a summer fling.

"You didn't talk to your father about what you saw?"

"I talked to Aunt Judith. When we got home, she could tell something was bothering me and took me out for ice cream."

Meghan's mouth went dry as dust. "You told her you saw your mother with another man?"

"Dad had already told her."

Or else, Meghan thought, Judith had only pretended to know in order to extract information. She'd witnessed firsthand the woman's finely honed manipulation skills. It wouldn't have been hard to convince a little boy that he wasn't telling her anything she didn't already know.

The barbed comments about the house and grounds that Judith frequently made bubbled from a hostility that still simmered below the surface. Twenty years later.

Judith refused to call her former sister-in-law by name and

her lips pursed to the size of a keyhole whenever her gaze settled on anything connected to Genevieve. And because almost everything on Blue Key Island in some way reflected the woman's creative, winsome personality, Cade's aunt walked around wearing an expression that looked as if she'd been sucking on lemons.

But how could she tell Cade her suspicions about Judith when he'd witnessed his mother's indiscretion with his own eyes?

His ten-year-old eyes...

"Are you sure you didn't misinterpret what you saw?" Meghan asked carefully. "Some people are more demonstrative than others. The embrace you saw could have been between...friends."

Cade stared at her. "I can't believe you're defending her actions."

"I'm only saying that it's possible what you saw might have been inappropriate...but innocent."

"If that was the case, I doubt my parents' marriage would have ended," he said stiffly.

It might have, Meghan thought grimly, with a little additional help.

She caught her bottom lip in her teeth, knowing she had nothing to base her beliefs on other than instinct. And instinct told her that Judith had poured her own special brand of acid into a weak spot in the Halloways' marriage and waited for it to dissolve.

"I don't know why Parker can't let go of the past and move on," Cade murmured. "I have."

"No, you haven't."

The eyebrow tried to put her in her place. Meghan ignored it. "Stuffing your emotions isn't the same as moving on."

"I don't…*stuff*…my emotions."

"Really? Then why do you drum?"

"Drum?"

Meghan glanced down meaningfully at his hands just as he caught himself, and his fingers stilled. "You drum because you won't express yourself in the way God designed you to express yourself. You need emotional Drano."

"And that would be?"

Meghan deposited her sketchbook in his lap and tucked the pencil between his fingers. "You're a smart guy. You figure it out."

Chapter Sixteen

A soft light glowed inside the studio but Meghan wasn't put off because she knew Bert left one burning all night. And everyone was at the house. All accounted for.

This was it. The last time she was going to look for the Ferris. Her assignment would be officially over. Mission... unaccomplished. But Meghan had decided she was fine with that. Large donation to Sidewalk Chalk or not, now that she'd gotten to know the Halloways, she was no longer comfortable working as Nina Bonnefield's undercover operative.

Meghan flipped the latch on the door and stepped inside.

"Oh—" *No.* Meghan backed up when she saw the man standing in the shadows. "I'm sorry. I didn't mean to intrude."

"You aren't intruding, Miss McBride," Douglas Halloway said. "Please. Come in."

Meghan hesitated but Cade's father waved her inside. "Sometimes an old man needs more than his own thoughts for company."

If Meghan hadn't heard the melancholy echo in Douglas's

voice, she would have been halfway back to the house by now. "You aren't old."

"The cast on my arm says differently."

"That could have happened to anyone. Young or old."

"Which means I'm clumsy." He sounded more disgruntled about that than being old.

"It means you're a beginner," Meghan corrected, bravely moving closer. "And you won't make the same mistake next time."

Douglas smiled and Meghan was amazed to see a tiny dent appear in his cheek. Why had she assumed it was Genevieve Halloway who'd passed on that appealing feature to her son?

"You're assuming there will be a next time. You know what they say. You can't teach an old dog new tricks."

"You don't believe that and neither do I." Amazed at her own temerity, Meghan braced herself for the fallout.

Instead, Douglas sighed. "Sometimes the evidence is too great to ignore. A man has to accept his successes. And his…failures."

Meghan got the distinct impression they were no longer talking about rock climbing. "But isn't it hard to discern sometimes which one is which? They can look the same, depending on your attitude."

"Has anyone ever told you that you're…astonishingly optimistic?"

"All the time," Meghan admitted. "But with a slight twist. *Annoyingly* optimistic seems to be the most popular choice of adjectives."

Douglas gave her a shrewd look and then shook his head, a slight smile playing at the corner of his lips. "Well, no wonder."

"No wonder what?" Meghan blinked, thoroughly confused by the cryptic remark.

But Douglas didn't reply. His gaze had already shifted to the paintings on the wall and Meghan realized it was riveted on the familiar watercolor of a man in a boat.

Cade must have moved the painting from his bedroom to the studio so he wouldn't have to look at it. Relief that he hadn't tossed it into the burn barrel mingled with frustration at another example of Cade's stubbornness.

"Cade is very gifted," she said softly.

Douglas made an undistinguishable sound that neither confirmed nor denied her comment. "He's the best in the firm. His designs have won several awards."

"I meant as an artist. He painted the one you're looking at, you know."

Douglas hadn't known. It was obvious in the way his eyes widened in surprise and then darkened. With what, though, Meghan couldn't discern. Denial? Anger? Regret?

Or maybe a combination of all three.

"I can't take the credit." Douglas flicked a look at the painting, his previous good humor evaporating like a drop of water in Bert's cast-iron skillet. "This was Nina's influence."

At the mention of the familiar name, Meghan sucked in a breath.

Was it possible Douglas was referring to Nina *Bonnefield?* Had she been one of the artists who'd encouraged Cade to paint?

Meghan sent up a quick prayer, appealing for wisdom. If she admitted she'd heard of Nina, a woman who claimed to live several thousand miles away on the east coast, Douglas might wonder how that was possible. In this case, anything she said had the potential to jump-start a game of Twenty Questions that Meghan didn't want to play. But if she didn't follow up on the comment, she'd lose the opportunity to find out more about her father's mysterious client.

"Who is Nina?" Meghan hoped that since Douglas had been the one to bring up the woman's name, he wouldn't read more into the question than simple curiosity.

Douglas remained silent for a moment and Meghan held her breath. His eyes never left the painting. "Nina is Cade's mother."

The two words liquefied Meghan's knees and she sagged against the wall. "His *mother?*"

Was it possible that Douglas had been married twice?

"I…I thought Genevieve was his mother's name."

A dark red stain crept up Douglas's cheeks and he looked away. "Nina is…*was*…a nickname."

A husband's affectionate, intimate nickname for his wife. That explained why Meghan hadn't heard anyone else use it until now.

Just as the ramifications of Douglas's stunning disclosure began to pile up, he forced a smile and shuffled past her, looking ten years older than he had a few minutes ago. "If you'll excuse me, I'm going back to the house. It's getting rather late."

Meghan could only nod. Because she had no idea what to say to him.

But she had plenty to say to her father.

Stumbling into the courtyard, Meghan punched a number on her cell phone and then hit the send button.

"Hello?" In spite of the lateness of the hour, Patrick McBride didn't sound sleepy or disoriented. That alone should have made her suspicious.

"Nina Bonnefield is Genevieve Halloway, Dad."

Silence.

"Did you hear me? Genevieve and Douglas divorced years

ago and she must have lost the estate in the settlement—"
Meghan suddenly realized she hadn't heard a surprised ex-
clamation. Or a horrified gasp. Nothing. Which could only
lead to one conclusion. One hive-inducing, nauseating,
instant insomnia-causing conclusion. "You…*knew.* Didn't
you?"

"I knew."

Meghan dropped her head between her knees and
groaned. *"Dad."*

"I promised Nina I'd keep that part confidential," Patrick
explained. "She assured me it would be simpler that way."

Simpler for who? Meghan was tempted to shout. She
groaned instead.

How could she begin to explain to her father that her assignment had been difficult enough when she believed Nina
Bonnefield had simply been one of Genevieve Halloway's
acquaintances? But knowing Nina was Cade's mother—the
woman he didn't bother to hide his bitterness for—added
complications she didn't have the time, energy or desire to
count at the moment.

Meghan stared blindly at the mosaic of colorful pottery
pieces cemented in the path stones beneath her feet.

"Meghan?" Patrick's worried voice broke through her
thoughts. "What's wrong? What's happened?"

What's happened?

Meghan had the strangest urge to laugh. And cry. What
should she tell him? That she'd befriended the runaway
bride? That she'd gotten way too attached to a place—and
people—she'd probably never see again? People who, if they
found out she'd come to the island under false pretenses,
might stop speaking to her?

Or that she'd fallen for the best man?

"I'm fine, Dad." Which at the moment was an acronym for *freaked out, insecure, neurotic and emotional.* "But you better tell me everything."

So he did. But by the time Patrick had finished, Meghan didn't feel any better. If it were possible, she felt worse.

According to Patrick, Parker had contacted her mother shortly after her engagement to Justin. Not only was Nina ecstatic to hear from her adult daughter, she was floored by Parker's shy declaration of her newfound faith. In Nina's own life, that phone call had been a life-changing affirmation that God really did listen. That He really did love her.

Because apparently, while Parker had been attending special evening services at her own church and feeling as though God was trying to get her attention, hundreds of miles away, He'd been nudging Genevieve, too. The gallery and café she managed had become the gathering place for a trio of women who stopped in for dessert and coffee after their weekly Bible study. Over the course of a few months, she'd overheard enough snippets of their lively discussions to get a new perspective on people who lived out their beliefs.

When she'd finally pulled out a chair at their table and asked them to explain it to her, it had been like finding a treasure.

Nina had begun her own faith journey, never dreaming it would ultimately connect with her daughter's.

When Patrick finished telling Meghan what he knew about Genevieve Halloway, Meghan still had no idea what to do. Or who to believe.

"Dad, Cade Halloway is convinced that Genevieve—*Nina*—had an affair with Joseph Ferris. And he told Parker about it today."

"What!" Patrick's dismay sounded genuine.

"I didn't want to believe it, either, but now I'm beginning

to wonder if it isn't true. I mean, it would explain why Joseph left a gift for her on the island."

"Nina told me that Ferris had been having some health problems and needed a quiet place to retreat. That's why he left something for her as a thank-you. She never mentioned anything about an affair."

"Maybe she thought you wouldn't help her if she told you everything."

They were silent, each of them absorbing the information they'd shared while trying to make sense of it.

The back of Meghan's head began to throb. She'd gone from defending Genevieve to doubting the woman's sincerity now that she knew who she really was.

"Did Nina tell you why she left?"

"No. Only that now she realizes she gave up much too easily."

Which could mean just about anything, Meghan thought grimly.

"I don't understand something. If Parker was open to meeting with Genevieve, then why did she send me here to look for the Ferris? Especially if the two of them were involved. If the family finds out, Genevieve has to know it's going to look as if the Ferris might be the real reason she's anxious to connect with Parker after so many years. Cade already believes she can't be trusted."

"Nina thought if you actually found the Ferris, she could show the family's lawyer the letter as proof and convince Douglas that it belonged to her. Then she planned to sell it for a down payment on the island. Parker had mentioned the island was going up for sale at the end of the summer. Nina said the house held so many memories, she didn't want to lose that connection to her family."

Tears burned the backs of Meghan's eyes when she realized what Genevieve had told Patrick closely paralleled what Parker had said about why she'd chosen the island for the wedding.

A grand gesture on Genevieve's part, Meghan thought, but it would still be suspect. And the timing couldn't have been worse.

Meghan exhaled. "You have to let Genevieve know that Cade told Parker about the affair before they talk again. As soon as possible."

"Ah—that might be a little difficult." Patrick paused and Meghan had a sudden image of him plucking off his glasses and wiping the lenses on his shirttail.

Dread curled in her belly. "Why will that be difficult?"

"Because she's on her way there—"

"What! She's coming here? Why?"

"Because someone sent Genevieve an invitation to the wedding."

"Dad? What are you doing up so late?" Cade paused in the kitchen doorway, surprised to see his father sitting alone at the table, a bowl piled high with Bert's leftover strawberry shortcake in front of him.

"I could ask you the same question."

Douglas could, Cade thought, but that didn't mean he had to answer it. Which in turn raised another interesting point. Why couldn't he and his father talk about anything that wasn't work-related?

"Have you talked to Parker?" Cade asked. He'd tried to approach his sister several times earlier in the afternoon but she'd stuck like glue to Bert or the teenage help, not giving him the chance to talk to her privately. Later on when he'd tried to seek her out, she was nowhere to be found.

"I haven't seen her since supper. But I did have a chat with your photographer friend. Meghan. She showed up at the studio."

Panic gripped Cade and he didn't even pause to wonder why his father had gone to the studio. "You talked to Meghan? About what?"

Instead of answering, Douglas aimed his spoon at an empty chair. "Sit down, son. You look a little tense."

Cade strode over and yanked the chair away from the table. "About what?" he repeated, hoping his father's abrasive personality hadn't roughed away a spot on Meghan's sensitive soul.

"About your artistic ability."

Cade winced. Wonderful. "I hope you weren't too hard on her, Dad. Meghan puts a high value on that—"

"It wasn't bad," Douglas interrupted. "The painting she said you did. Not as good as Nina's, of course, but not half bad."

Cade, who hadn't heard his father utter Genevieve's name in years, was momentarily stunned into silence.

"You quit, didn't you?"

Cade wondered if it was a trick question. A week ago the answer would have been a decisive yes. But today, the charcoal sketch of the eagle he'd drawn after Meghan left him at the point could be entered as evidence against him.

"Work keeps me busy. I don't have time for anything else." Douglas couldn't fault him for that. Not when he'd modeled Douglas's own intense brand of dedication to the firm all these years.

Instead of getting an approving nod, Douglas frowned at him. "There's more to life than work, Cade."

The berries in Bert's shortcake had obviously fermented. "Excuse me?"

"I was thinking this evening that maybe we shouldn't rush into selling this place," Douglas mused. "It might be a good place to retire."

"You want to retire. Here." Cade pinched the bridge of his nose between his fingers as the opening music to a popular old sci-fi series played in his head.

"I don't know. I'm just weighing my options."

"You can find something closer. Up by the boundary waters. This place is beyond repair—"

"Is it, do you think? Beyond repair?" The look of deep regret on his father's face cut off Cade's opening argument.

The two men stared at each other across the table.

The chair creaked in protest as Cade shifted his weight. "We haven't been here in twenty years, Dad. Why are we holding on to it? The yard is a scrap heap. The house is falling apart. Selling the island is a sound business decision. You agreed with me. I don't know why everyone gets so sentimental about it. Blue Key is just the place…" Cade bit back the words that had forged ahead of his thoughts.

"Go ahead and say it," Douglas prompted softly.

"All right. The place where Mom had an affair with Joseph Ferris that ended your marriage." Finally being able to say the words out loud didn't feel as good as Cade thought it would. "Or am I the only one who remembers that? She made a mockery of everything about this place."

"You can't put all the blame on Genevieve." Douglas sighed. "I made my share of mistakes."

"What mistake? Marrying a flighty artist who got tired of her life and changed it as easily as she painted over a canvas? 'I didn't get it right, so I guess I'll start over with someone else…'"

"Cade?"

Meghan's voice barely broke a whisper but he heard her. And when he saw her chalk-white face, he rose to his feet so quickly the chair almost overturned. "What's wrong?"

"I'm sorry to interrupt, but I need to…talk to you."

Cade glanced at his father. "Dad?"

"Of course." Douglas smiled reassuringly at Meghan but when he would have risen to his feet, she shook her head.

"Both of you."

"All right." Cade reached for her hand but she skirted away from him and went to stand by the sink. A cold trickle of unease skittered down his spine. "What's going on?"

"It's about…Genevieve. You need to know that she's on her way here…someone sent her an invitation to the wedding."

"Parker." Cade closed his eyes, wondering how, in spite of his best efforts, life had gotten so out of control. He looked at Douglas, ready for the fireworks. "I'm sorry, Dad. I should have told you that she contacted Mom, but I had no idea she would invite her to the wedding—"

"Parker didn't invite her," Douglas interrupted. "I did."

For the second time Cade felt as if he'd been sucker punched. "Why would you do that?"

"This is her daughter's wedding. Nina would want to be here. She *should* be here."

Anger warred with disbelief. "Don't you think after twenty years, she gave up her right to be included? She's the one who left *us*." As soon as Cade voiced his thoughts out loud, Meghan's soft admonition about people deserving second chances tweaked his conscience.

Right behind that tweak came the humbling realization that she was right. Where would he be if God hadn't forgiven him? If he wanted to live out his beliefs, forgiveness was a good place to start.

"I think this is a good time for us to join this family meeting." Parker's shaky voice interrupted her father and she nudged the woman standing rigidly beside her. "After you."

Before Cade had a chance to react, Meghan slipped past them and left the room. He would have followed her but his sister's stricken expression held him in place.

"Dad? Aunt Judith has something to tell you."

Chapter Seventeen

Cade stepped out into the courtyard and the breeze touched his face, carrying a hint of perfume from the flower gardens. He stared with unseeing eyes into the darkness until he felt someone beside him.

Parker linked her arm through his.

"No offense, but I'd like to be alone." He kept his voice even, careful not to let any emotion leach into it.

"That's why you shouldn't be." Parker leaned against him but Cade had the strangest feeling that his sister was offering *her* strength, not seeking his. "What do you think they're talking about?"

"Dad and Judith? After what happened tonight, I wouldn't begin to take a guess."

"I want to be angry with her but I feel...I don't know. Numb." Parker sighed. "I didn't believe Mom had had an affair with Joseph Ferris, but until I confronted Aunt Judith and asked her what she knew about Mom leaving, I never would have guessed she was capable of such coldhearted... *deception.* She still thinks she did the right thing. She threatened Mom because she was convinced we were all better off without her."

Cade swallowed hard against the knot in his throat. The one that had formed during his aunt's self-righteous tirade and showed no signs of easing. "An institution. Mom." He could hardly put the two words in the same sentence. "And she wasn't even mentally ill."

"I think in her heart Mom believed she wasn't a good wife and mother. And she was so sensitive, it made her even more susceptible to Judith's threats," Parker said softly. "Don't you remember how hard Judith was on Mom? How she made it seem as if Mom had some flaw in her personality because she marched to a different drummer? I'd guess that Mom was afraid Judith was right in believing something was wrong with her. She forgot to pick us up from school sometimes. She must have thought she was a disappointment to Dad because she wasn't a typical country-club wife. And then her relationship with Ferris became suspect."

That's when Judith had seen an opportunity and struck.

Cade closed his eyes but could still see his aunt standing in the kitchen just minutes ago, logically and coolly stating "her side" of the situation. Supremely confident that neither her brother nor the children she'd practically raised as her own could fault her for what she'd done.

The fact that Judith firmly believed Genevieve wasn't a fit parent and had taken steps to cut her sister-in-law off from the family only made the circumstances surrounding Genevieve's abrupt departure more terrible.

All three of the Halloways had listened to Judith's confession with a growing sense of horror. And for the first time, Cade had a glimpse of what his sensitive, vulnerable mother had gone through. Not only day-to-day but following that last visit to the island.

According to Judith, after they'd returned to Minneapolis, Judith sensed the tension in the household and had gotten Cade to confide in her about what had happened. To a woman who prided herself on her family's spotless reputation, it had been the last straw. She'd told Genevieve to leave. And she'd warned her that if she refused, she knew the family doctor would confirm it was his opinion Genevieve was suffering from borderline personality disorder.

Genevieve had left to save the family from embarrassment. And the fact that she'd given up without a fight proved that she believed there was something innately wrong with her.

Cade had a hunch that Parker was right. Judith's threat must have triggered Genevieve's own insecurities and she was afraid the stigma of being institutionalized—even for a short time—would hurt Douglas's reputation and have a profound affect on her children.

In the end, Genevieve had walked away. Not from them. But *for* them.

As the weight of that realization sank in, Cade wondered bleakly if their family could ever recover.

"Cade? Will you pray with me?" Parker's uncertain voice cut through his pain.

"I'm not sure what to say," he admitted in a husky voice.

"Just say what's on your mind. And in your heart."

Cade closed his eyes again as his sister took his hand. For a moment he struggled to find the right words. Freedom came when he realized that God didn't wait until he found them… He met him right where he was at.

* * *

"I think I hear a boat. Do you think it's Justin?" Parker lurched toward the window but Meghan grabbed her shoulders and held her in place.

"Hold still or you're going to pop a button on your gown. Remember, this kind of thing is Bliss Markham's forte, not mine." Meghan turned Parker toward the mirror again and their eyes met. Parker's were still red rimmed and puffy; Meghan's shadowed from a sleepless night. They shared a wan smile, silently acknowledging a promise to make the day ahead a celebration in spite of what had happened the night before.

"Bliss," Parker scoffed, stretching up on her tiptoes to try to see out the window. "If you switched careers, you'd give her a run for her money."

Meghan shuddered at the thought of being a full-time event planner. "I'll stick to critters, thank you very much. Now, go ahead and breathe."

Parker obeyed, although she didn't seem nearly as interested in what she looked like in her wedding gown as she did about the boat chugging up to the dock. "It's Bert's fault my dress feels a little tight. I can't say no to her buttermilk pancakes."

Meghan smiled. Parker looked beautiful. Her dress had arrived via special courier—namely Verne Thatcher—and she'd discarded the elaborate veil for a tiny cluster of wild roses tucked in her chignon. Justin's arrival had been delayed for a day due to an emergency meeting with his sponsoring church but Meghan hoped he'd be on the island soon. Although Parker had confided that she'd called him during the middle of the night, Meghan knew she needed the reassurance of his presence.

Bert had the reception well in hand, which left Meghan to continue her role as wedding planner. She'd ruthlessly put her own emotions aside in order to concentrate on Parker and Justin's wedding day.

"I have to see if it's Justin. He promised he'd be here right after lunch. Or maybe it's some of the kids from Willoughby."

In a generous display of hospitality, Parker had invited all the teenagers who'd helped clear and decorate the courtyard to the wedding.

"If you promise to stay put, I'll look."

"I promise." Parker fidgeted but only her eyes moved as she watched Meghan walk to the window.

Of course Cade had to be the first person that Meghan saw. Her heart constricted as she watched him stride down the narrow cobblestone path to the lake.

He wore a black tuxedo and a satin cummerbund over a crisp white shirt. Not rented, of course, but custom fit for his tall, lean frame. The breeze ruffled his dark hair and his set profile gave her no hints as to what was going on inside his head. Or his heart.

He hadn't made an appearance at breakfast, a subdued affair since Judith had opted to leave the island early that morning. Parker had confided in Meghan that she had no idea what her father had said to her aunt, but she'd intercepted her on her way out the door and encouraged her to stay for the wedding. Parker's willingness to forgive was a testimony to her deepening faith and—although Meghan didn't comment on it out loud—another affirmation that she and Justin would accomplish amazing things together for God.

After Meghan had left the family alone in the kitchen the night before, she'd grabbed a flashlight and made her way to the point to pray. She'd prayed for healing for the entire family. And she'd prayed for Judith.

By the time she'd returned to the house, there was only one light burning. In Cade's room. More than anything, Meghan had wanted to find out how he was doing. What he was feeling. And she might have summoned the courage to tap on his door if she hadn't remembered what he'd said about Genevieve.

She couldn't deny the attraction between them. And the kiss they almost shared in Willoughby told her that Cade felt it, too. But if Meghan had dared to hope the fragile threads of friendship could turn into something stronger—something lasting—it was crushed when she'd heard Cade disdainfully dismiss his mother as a flighty artist.

If she kept their relationship from progressing, he wouldn't get close enough to see the "real" Meghan. If she kept her distance, she could hide the things that he would see as flaws. And she wouldn't die a little inside every time he rolled his eyes in frustration. Or flash an impatient look at her when she misplaced her camera. Or her purse. Or her car keys. Or all three.

"Can you see who it is?" Parker's voice yanked her back to the present.

"Just a—" Meghan's voice died in her throat as she saw Cade pause as he reached the end of the dock. Her gaze shifted to the small motor boat and then settled on the person climbing out of it.

Not Justin. A woman. Tall. Slender. With a straw hat perched on her dark hair; the jaunty yellow flower fastened to the brim a perfect match to the formfitting satin sheath she wore. It wasn't until she swept off the hat and used it as a fan that Meghan saw the marked resemblance to Parker.

Genevieve.

Meghan sucked in a breath, recognizing the split second when mother and son recognized one another. Cade remained frozen while Genevieve stood poised on the dock, like a bird ready to take flight.

Please, God.

They were the only words her thoughts could form as she watched.

Cade took a few hesitant steps forward and held out his hand to help her from the boat. Genevieve took it and pressed it against her cheek. Meghan felt a tear slip down her cheek as Cade wrapped his arms around Genevieve and rocked her in his arms, as if she were the child and he were the parent.

"Meghan? Who is it? Is it Justin?"

"It's your mother," she whispered.

"I now pronounce you husband and wife. You may kiss the bride."

Cade averted his eyes—Parker was still his baby sister, after all—and his gaze moved to Meghan, who was snapping a picture of the couple's embrace.

She had stayed in the background for most of the day, catching candid shots of last-minute preparations and capturing moments of what the Society pages would no longer title "The Wedding of the Summer."

But the small gathering of people didn't seem to care that there was no orchestra, just the music provided by a temperamental fountain that had gurgled to life shortly before the ceremony started. Or that the elaborate six-course dinner had been replaced with simple hors d'oeuvres. Or that a frisky bichon was one of the guests.

The only thing that had shaken things up a bit was when

Douglas walked into the courtyard with Genevieve on his arm. And they stood side by side as Parker and Justin recited their vows.

When Cade had seen Genevieve, the years had melted away. And so had his anger. Maybe he'd never totally understand everything that had happened, but he'd suddenly realized it didn't matter anymore. When he saw the uncertainty, and the hope, in his mother's eyes—eyes the exact shade of blue as his—he'd realized Meghan was right. There was a time to forgive and start over. A time to make room for people in your life.

He'd spent a lot of time talking to God and knew he'd no longer be satisfied with a faith confined to an hour on Sunday morning.

Once again, Cade's eyes drifted to Meghan, who was laughing as she knelt down to snap a picture of Miss Molly.

She was beautiful.

When the excitement surrounding the wedding ebbed, he planned to tell Meghan how he felt. About his desire to pursue a closer relationship with God—and with her.

Chapter Eighteen

For ten minutes Cade tried unsuccessfully to get past Caitlin McBride's receptionist. The young woman's curly blond hair and wide brown eyes made her look as good-natured and easygoing as a golden retriever puppy, but Cade had quickly discovered looks were deceiving. She was part guard dog. And she wasn't about to let him into the inner sanctum without an appointment.

It appeared that Caitlin's receptionist was either deathly afraid of the consequences of breaking company policy or else she… Cade noticed the panic in her eyes. No. She was deathly afraid of the consequences.

She seemed more afraid of angering her employer than keeping a potential client happy. Which made him rethink his decision to approach Meghan's older sister. But only for a split second. At this point, he was getting desperate.

"Listen, Miss—"

"Buckley."

"Miss Buckley. If you'll just let Caitlin know I'm here, I'm sure she'll see me. I'm a…friend of the family."

"What did you say your name was?"

He hadn't said. "I'd like to surprise her."

Miss Buckley's eyes narrowed. "If you're a friend of the family, you'd know Miss McBride doesn't like surprises."

Cade tamped down his frustration. "Fine. I'll make an appointment. When is she available?"

He hoped it would be before lunch.

"Let me check." Miss Buckley turned to the computer and her fingers danced lightly across the keyboard. "The first week of November. What time works best for you?"

"November. You've got to be kidding me. Does everyone in this city have such low self-esteem that they have to—"

"Thank you, Sabrina." A terse but feminine voice interrupted him. "I have a few minutes to speak with Mr. Halloway before my nine-thirty."

Cade turned and saw a woman standing just inside the foyer, holding a disposable cup of coffee in each hand.

A woman who'd immediately known who he was even though he was sure they'd never been introduced.

Cade searched vainly for a genetic link that would identify her as Meghan's sister and couldn't come up with a match. Meghan, with her wild mass of curls, winsome smile and penchant for jeans and T-shirts had nothing in common with the serious, cool-eyed woman impeccably dressed in a pencil-thin black skirt, silk blouse and stiletto heels.

Maybe she was Caitlin's personal assistant….

"Of course, Miss McBride."

Or not.

Sabrina Buckley bobbed her head diffidently, as if addressing royalty. Cade half expected the secretary to curtsy.

"Follow me." Caitlin barely spared him a glance as she

swept past, pausing long enough to deposit one of the cups on the reception desk.

Cade followed her to the office suite at the end of the hall but once she ushered him inside and closed the door, he was suddenly at a loss. A feeling he wasn't used to experiencing.

Caitlin didn't offer him a seat. Instead she remained standing and folded her arms across her chest. Waiting for him to make the next move.

But Cade was through playing games.

"Meghan won't return my calls," he said with blunt honesty. "I've stopped by the studio but she doesn't keep regular hours. When I called the minister who coordinates Sidewalk Chalk, he told me that Meghan had asked for a month off."

"Really." Caitlin didn't sound surprised.

"I have to talk to her."

"It doesn't sound like she wants to talk to you."

"She just thinks she doesn't," he muttered.

A fleeting smile skimmed across her face. So fleeting that Cade knew he must have imagined it. "I can't help you."

"Why not?"

"Because my sister is miserable. And I'm still trying to decide if it's because she let you into her life or because you're not part of it anymore."

For some strange reason, finding out Meghan was miserable made Cade feel a whole lot better. "I messed up. Big-time."

Caitlin's perfectly shaped eyebrow lifted in a tell-me-something-I-don't-know gesture.

"It would help if I…" For a split second Cade's pride tried to muzzle him. He hated to admit the truth. Especially to a woman who was already eyeing him as if he were a smear on a microscope slide.

But really, Cade asked himself, what did he have to lose? Meghan.

Which translated to *everything*.

So he told the truth. "It would help if I knew *why* she won't talk to me."

Caitlin stared at him in disbelief. "You really don't know why?"

"Totally clueless."

"Talk to my sister."

"I would love to talk to your sister," Cade pointed out with exaggerated patience. "But I can't. That's why I was hoping *you'd* talk to me. Explain what's going on."

"You want closure."

"I want Meghan," Cade snapped.

Caitlin's shoulders stiffened, encouraging Cade to clarify the statement. Quickly. "I…care about her. I have to apologize and tell her how I feel."

Caitlin's gaze shifted, as if talking about emotions was uncomfortable for her.

Silence weighted the air between them and Cade waited, half expecting her to show him the door. She didn't. Instead, in a gesture that struck Cade as oddly vulnerable, she pushed her lower lip out and blew a sigh, stirring the wisp of bangs on her forehead.

"You can *tell* her, Cade," she finally said. "But getting her to *believe* you—that's going to be the tough part."

"Why wouldn't she believe me?"

"I don't know." Caitlin splayed her fingers and studied her French manicure. "Maybe because you disapproved of your sister marrying Justin. Or because you said your mother couldn't be trusted because she's a flighty artist. Or because—correct me if I'm wrong here—you label your tools and, if asked, you could find the receipt for the first Rolex you bought. In less than five minutes."

Meghan had obviously confided in her sister. Cade wasn't sure where to file that one on his pros and cons list.

"I think Parker and Justin make a great couple. I was being stupid when I described my mother as flighty. She's actually incredibly amazing. And I'm not sure what the rest of what you said has to do with anything." Frustration leached into Cade's voice. "Doesn't everyone keep receipts?"

Caitlin's expression softened for the first time. "Not Megs. She manages to lose them in her purse on the way home from the store. She can be a little…unorganized."

Cade thought the assessment unfair. "She orchestrated my sister's entire wedding reception. Kept my aunt Judith in line. Supervised a group of rowdy teenagers." *And bullied me into painting again.*

"I know she did." Caitlin regarded him levelly. "That doesn't mean she wasn't out of her comfort zone. Or her galaxy, from the way she described it."

"Meghan seemed to thrive on all the commotion."

"'Seemed to' being the key words."

Cade didn't follow. "What are you getting at?"

"I'm not sure I should bother, considering you claim to care about Meghan and yet you don't know anything about her. I'll give you the benefit of the doubt, though, because Megs is a pro at masking her feelings. She helped with the wedding because it meant a lot to Parker, not because she, to borrow your word, thrives on activity. Her faith held her together, but I'll bet she found a place to hide and recharge."

"She—" Did. The argument Cade was ready to present disintegrated. His fists clenched at his sides. From the look in Caitlin's eyes, there was more. He also knew she wasn't sure she could trust him.

But he was running out of options. The only bridge between him and Meghan was Evie or Caitlin McBride. He would have preferred Evie, the nurturing junior high teacher. Instead he was at the mercy of another nail-chewing, first-born overachiever. Someone a lot like himself.

Parker was right. God did have a sense of humor.

"Tell me the rest." He added the magic word. "Please."

"I better not regret this." Caitlin gave him a hard look. "If I had to guess, I'd say my sister thinks you wouldn't be able to deal with her ADD."

"Her what?"

"Attention deficit disorder."

Cade frowned. "Isn't that a kid thing?"

"That's what people hear about the most, but adults have it, too. Sometimes children outgrow it and sometimes they don't. Megs didn't. We didn't even realize she had ADD until she was in college. Evie had picked the topic for a term paper and during her research she realized Meghan had all the classic signs."

"That's the reason why she won't return my calls?" It didn't make sense to him.

"It hasn't been easy for her, but Meghan works *with* it. She designed her life—her interests and her career—to play to her strengths." Caitlin paused and met his gaze directly. "And she's just as careful when it comes to her relationships."

Cade sank into the leather chair opposite Caitlin's desk without permission as the enormity of her meaning began to sink in. For the first time he had a clear picture of the damage he'd unknowingly inflicted on Meghan over and over again with his careless words. Now he understood why she'd left so abruptly after the wedding. And why she'd rebuffed his attempts to contact her.

"Wow." Cade closed his eyes, bracketing his face with his hands. When he drew a careful breath, it felt as if someone had slid a knife between his ribs.

"Exactly." The sympathetic note in Caitlin's voice scared him more than her anger.

He opened his eyes and his gaze locked with hers. "So what do I do now?"

"Give up?"

"Not an option." And there was no way he was going to apologize for that.

"I'm not sure you understand. She's always going to struggle with attention issues, Cade. This isn't something that she can make go away if she tries hard enough. And for the record, I haven't seen her struggle with her self-esteem like this since she was first diagnosed. I'm sure you get the credit for that."

Cade absorbed the hit, knowing it originated from Caitlin's loyalty and love for her sister. He wouldn't expect anything less.

"There's something between us." Cade waited to see if Meghan's sister would deny it.

She didn't. Which fanned a tiny flame of hope inside of him.

"Megs is afraid she'd drive you crazy in less than a month."

"Does she drive *you* crazy?" Cade had a strong hunch Meghan's sister not only alphabetized her spices, but also her cleaning supplies and the paperback novels on her bookshelf.

"Of course she does." Caitlin grinned, and for the first time Cade saw the marked resemblance between the two sisters. Unguarded, Caitlin's smile was every bit as charming as

Meghan's. "But she knows I love her exactly the way she is. She's Megs. I wouldn't want her to change."

"So, you're going to convince her to talk to me?"

"I already tried," Caitlin admitted, stunning Cade into silence. "But she doesn't see the point. She isn't being stubborn—she's protecting her heart."

From him.

Maybe it was too late to patch things up. She'd taken a month's hiatus from the ministry she poured her heart and soul into. Thanks to him, she was struggling once again with accepting the way God had designed her. He wouldn't let that one go without a fight. Not when she'd been the one who'd challenged him to seek out a deeper relationship with God.

"How do I get in touch with her?"

"You must be a glutton for punishment."

"She can kick me out after I apologize for being an…" He searched for the right words.

"Arrogant jerk," Caitlin supplied.

"Thanks," Cade said dryly. "That about sums it up."

Caitlin seemed to make a decision. "Megs is out of town on a shoot for the rest of the week, taking photos of birds at a wildlife rehabilitation center for their brochure. But she *might* have mentioned something about visiting a friend on an island before she comes back to the Cities."

"She's going to Blue Key?" Cade couldn't believe it.

"I doubt she meant Hawaii."

He wasn't intimidated by the cool response. In fact, Cade was so "not intimidated" that he crossed the distance between them, framed her face in his hands and planted a light kiss on her smooth forehead. "I owe you, Caitlin."

"Just don't mess up. If I have to intervene again, I'm going to charge you a hundred and twenty dollars an hour."

Chapter Nineteen

Meghan shaded her eyes against the sun as Verne's fishing boat skipped over the waves toward the island. The maple trees already flashed bits of scarlet and gold high in the green of their branches, reminding Meghan of a Scottish plaid.

A little over a month ago, she'd caught her first glimpse of the main house and fallen instantly in love.

The house wasn't the only thing you fell in love with.

She shook the thought away before it left a mark on her heart.

Maybe she was crazy to come back to Blue Key so soon, but Bert had insisted she spend the weekend when Meghan had mentioned she'd be in the area on a shoot.

"Someone expecting you?" Verne called over the growl of the motor.

The question was almost identical to the one he'd asked her the first time she'd arrived; tears sprang into Meghan's eyes. She hoped Verne would attribute them to the wind.

"Bert knows I'm coming over."

Verne cut the motor and guided the boat along the dock.

Smith and Wesson stirred at her feet and raised their noses, sensing the change in direction.

The fishing guide picked up Meghan's duffel bag but this time he deposited it on the dock as carefully as a bellhop handling a Gucci bag at the Ritz.

"I'll be back when you give me a jingle."

"I'm leaving Sunday afternoon. One o'clock. Remember?"

"You may decide to stay longer." He gave Meghan a cheerful wink as he grasped her elbow and helped her out of the boat.

"One o'clock—"

The motor drowned out the rest of the words as Verne revved it up for the return trip.

Two days on Blue Key Island would be more than enough. Meghan hadn't stepped on dry land yet and already memories of Cade were crowding in. It occurred to her that she'd run away from him and ended up in the very place they'd met.

Way to think things through, Meghan, she chided herself.

For several weeks she'd dodged his repeated attempts to get in touch with her.

Deleting the messages he'd left on her answering machine, both at the studio and on her cell phone, had taken more strength than stepping into Bliss Markham's shoes. But when she'd happened to see his name added to the list of volunteers for the next Sidewalk Chalk mural, she'd promptly requested some time off. The shoot she'd just finished had been an answer to her frantic prayers for a reprieve.

She hadn't realized that cutting Cade out of her life would feel like undergoing open heart surgery—without an anesthetic.

It's for the best, she reminded herself. Maybe there'd been a slight attraction between them, but nothing that her many quirks couldn't snuff out in record time.

Meghan swung the strap of her duffel bag over her shoulder, scanning the beach to see if Miss Molly had heard the boat pull up to the dock.

There was no sign of the dog or her owner.

Walking up the path, she heard music coming from the courtyard and cut through the sculpture garden to follow it to its source.

The wedding decorations had been taken down but Meghan could still picture the way everything had looked that day. Parker and Justin standing under the rose arbor, holding hands as they recited the vows they'd written. Genevieve and Douglas standing side by side in honor of their daughter, each little glance that passed between them uncertain yet cautiously optimistic.

Parker had left a message on Meghan's answering machine right before she and Justin had left for their honeymoon, letting her know that her parents had met for dinner—alone—several days after the wedding.

Judith had moved out of the family mansion and bought a condo of her own in an upscale neighborhood near the river. She'd also made a sizable contribution to Justin and Parker's ministry fund. It was Parker's theory that that was as close to an apology as Judith would ever make for what she'd done.

Meghan had no idea what was going to happen between Douglas and Genevieve. But whatever it was, she did know that God could help them reclaim those lost years when they'd let their insecurities drive their actions.

God, she knew, was very good at putting broken things

back together. Piece by piece, He was doing the same thing in her life, too.

Maybe by the time she was eighty years old, her heart would look the way it had before she'd met Cade.

She followed the neatly groomed path around the side of the house and stopped as abruptly as if she'd hit an invisible wall.

Water bubbled from the mermaid fountain, catching the sunlight and creating a muted rainbow that fanned across the stones.

The summer flowers had faded a bit, replaced by pale peach mums that bloomed along the foundation. Asters had escaped the ornate Victorian fence and popped up in the courtyard, spilling across the ground to the…carousel.

Meghan blinked.

Someone had begun the painstaking process of restoring it. The knight's steed already sported a fresh coat of ebony paint.

The carousel was obviously going up for sale along with the rest of Genevieve's collection. It was the only reason Meghan could think of to explain the makeover.

Discouragement weighted her steps as she moved closer to get a better look. She felt a little bit better when she realized that whoever had been hired to do the restoration was definitely qualified. In the interest of time, some artists would have simply chosen one color for the detailing. This one had accented the intricate medallions on the saddle and bridle with gold. Every decorative swirl and whorl on the crest of the chest plate had been meticulously highlighted with the sweep of a number four brush.

Meghan reached out and traced the arch of the horse's head with her fingers, wishing she could scrape up the money to buy the carousel and relocate it to a green space for the kids to enjoy.

A sharp bark came from the woods and she looked up just in time to see Miss Molly break out of the undergrowth.

"Hey, you." Laughing, Meghan scooped the dog up in her arms and cuddled her. "Where's Bert?"

Miss Molly barked a reply that Meghan couldn't decipher and squirmed frantically in her arms. That Meghan understood. She wanted down.

She set the dog back down. "Go find her. Go find Bert."

Amazingly enough, Miss Molly disappeared the way she'd come. When she returned moments later, the person who stepped out of the woods behind her wasn't Bert.

It was Cade.

Meghan's traitorous senses absorbed his familiar features like a dry sea sponge. He looked different somehow and she realized it was the first time she'd ever seen him wearing a pair of blue jeans that had seen better days and a worn-out cotton sweater, the sleeves pushed up to his elbows.

She wanted to run away but her feet wouldn't cooperate. By the time she got her bearings, he was standing in front of her, his eyes searching her face. Looking for something.

Meghan turned away, afraid he'd be able to read what was in her heart.

"So, what do you think about the carousel?" Cade asked, pushing his hands casually into his back pockets. As if they hadn't been apart for almost two months. As if she shouldn't find it strange that he was on the island, too.

"It looks good." Meghan tried to match his tone.

"Thanks." Cade grinned. "I think."

Realization slammed into her. "*You're* the one restoring it?"

"Yup. Someone suggested that I stop…ah, plugging up my

creative outlet. I discovered that restoration satisfies my somewhat scary need for precision and order, and also keeps me from drumming my fingers."

Meghan tried to suppress a smile as the memory of that afternoon on the point slipped into her thoughts.

"Don't," Cade said quietly.

"Don't what?"

"Try to forget. I haven't been able to."

Meghan swallowed hard. "I suppose you're here to get things ready for the sale."

"We decided to hang on to the place. Parker and Justin need a place to stay when they come back on furlough…and Bert let Mom talk her into opening up the studio to the locals for beginning art classes. Dad is determined he's going to take up fishing when he retires. And this project will keep me busy for quite a while. Unless I can convince someone to help me. Do you know anyone who might be interested?"

"Cade—" Meghan took a step back. This was too hard. She had to make up an excuse and leave before he caused irreparable damage to her heart.

"Come on. I have something to show you." Cade took her hand before she could escape and led her toward the house.

"Where's Bert?" Panicked, Meghan looked around for an ally. All she saw was Miss Molly, who'd been won over to Cade's side long ago.

"She's working, but she said she'll see you at dinner."

"Dinner…" That was hours from now.

"It'll only take a minute. Please."

Meghan couldn't resist the please. She gave in and let him tow her into the house and up the stairs to the bedroom she'd stayed in.

He nudged her over to the window and pushed aside the curtain.

Meghan shifted her weight to the other foot but she could still feel the warmth of Cade's skin through the thin cotton shirt he wore. One slight turn and she'd be in his arms...

"Genevieve told me the real reason you came here."

It was the last thing she expected him to say but she shouldn't have been surprised. Is that why he'd been trying to get in touch with her? To chew her out for her trying to help his mother find the Ferris?

Meghan moistened her lips. "I stopped looking for it. I didn't feel right considering how I felt about—" *You.* "Your family. Dad gets involved in these crazy schemes sometimes and—"

"Meghan?" Cade interrupted softly. "Look down."

Confused, Meghan obeyed. "What—"

And then she saw it.

The colorful mosaic of stones that circled the courtyard—the ones they'd spent hours weeding—took on a new shape. They formed an intricate network around the fountain, the colors shifting like a rainbow from pale to bright.

"Cade—I can't believe..." Meghan swallowed. "Do you really think..." She couldn't finish a sentence.

Cade understood. "Ferris. It had to be. Mom loved her gardens—it would have been a fitting gift to create something he knew she'd treasure. But Mom never came back to Blue Key and Ferris moved to Italy at the end of the summer. He sent her one letter, explaining his sister would be taking care of him during his illness and telling her he'd left a gift for her. Mom never told him about the accusations or the divorce—she didn't want to add to his burdens." Cade's voice was husky. "You were right. What I saw that day was my mother comforting a person who'd just told her that he'd been diagnosed with cancer. They were more acquaintances than friends. Definitely not lovers."

Meghan's throat closed at the easy way Cade referred to Genevieve as "Mom." "What about Bert? Didn't she know?"

"Bert didn't move to the island until the following summer, so she never questioned who'd created the mosaic. She was just as shocked as I was when I showed it to her."

"But how did you find it?" Meghan had spent a week in the room. She'd looked out the window several times a day and never noticed the thing she'd been searching for had been literally right under her nose.

Cade braced his fingers on the window frame and stared down at the courtyard. "The truth? I was standing right here a few days ago, praying for wisdom. Because I knew you were going to be here and I was wondering how I could ever get you to agree to be in the same room with me after I'd hurt you. When I opened my eyes, I saw it. Plain as day."

Meghan turned blindly away, rejecting the words. She couldn't read too much into them…couldn't imagine what they might mean.

Cade's voice stopped her as she reached the door.

"You told my sister that if she believed God had brought her and Justin together, she shouldn't let her fear keep them apart. Are you sure that isn't what you're doing?"

It wasn't fair, Meghan decided. He'd known she was coming and he'd gathered all his ammunition beforehand. "I'm not going to fit into your life. Maybe for a little while we could make it work, but eventually…" It would kill her if he got impatient with her. Got tired of her.

"You can leave but you aren't going to get rid of me that

easily. If I have to adopt a whole litter of little puff balls to get you to spend time with me, I will."

Meghan's mouth dropped open. "Parker told you that I'm a pet photographer."

"Actually, it was Caitlin."

"Caitlin?" Meghan choked. "You talked to my sister?"

"And lived to tell about it," Cade said, a glint of humor in his eyes. "She's the one who told me you'd be here this weekend. And if I'm not mistaken, it was her way of giving us her blessing."

Her blessing…

"You don't understand." She would have explained when their eyes caught and held. What she saw in his stripped the air from her lungs.

"I understand that I said stupid things that hurt you. I understand that I need *you*, Meghan." Cade advanced slowly, crossing the distance between them until they were inches apart. "I understand that my life is a gray, boring…cubicle… without you. I have no idea what *you'd* be getting out of the relationship, but I'll make you a promise. When you need time alone, I'll guard the path to the point so no one gets past. And I'll *always* help you find your camera."

Meghan choked back a sob. "How can a girl refuse an offer like that?"

"I'm hoping it's too good to pass up." Cade brushed his thumb against a tear that ran down her cheek.

"It is."

Cade exhaled slowly, closed his eyes and drew her against him as carefully as if she were made of glass. "What a relief," he murmured in her ear. "Because I was really hoping I wouldn't have to get those puppies."

Meghan's hiccup turned into a laugh as she breathed in the

scent of him. Felt the strength of his arms around her. It felt a lot like coming home.

"Meghan?"

"Mmm?"

"If you let me kiss you, I'll let you drive the boat."

She smiled up at him. "It's a deal."

* * * * *

*In November 2008, be sure to read Caitlin's story,
FAMILY TREASURES. Available from Kathryn
Springer and Steeple Hill Love Inspired.*

Dear Reader,

Eagles may be a common sight here in northern Wisconsin, but seeing one never fails to take my breath away! And they are a beautiful reminder of Isaiah 40:31. Many times in my own life, when I've felt stretched beyond what I think I can endure, I've leaned on the promise in this verse:

"…those who hope in the Lord will renew their strength. They will soar on wings like eagles…"

But in order to soar, you have to let go and leave the safety of the nest! As Meghan and Cade discovered, God sometimes nudges His children out of their comfort zones. It isn't always easy to trust in those instances, but it can result in a deeper relationship with Him…and with each other.

I hope you enjoyed getting to know Meghan. Be sure to watch for Caitlin's story, FAMILY TREASURES, in November. The oldest McBride sister is about to meet her match!

Blessings,

Kathryn Springer

QUESTIONS FOR DISCUSSION

1. What was your first impression of Meghan? Of Cade? How did their backgrounds influence the way they viewed life?

2. Cade claimed that selling Blue Key Island was a good business decision. What was really at the root of his decision?

3. Do you have a special "retreat" where you go to think or to pray? What is it like? Where is it?

4. Both Meghan and Cade had some trust issues. What were they based on? How were they alike and how did they differ?

5. How did Parker's growing faith challenge Cade's relationship with God? What influence did Meghan's faith have on him?

6. Meghan felt as if she were out of her "comfort zone" when she helped with Parker Halloway's wedding. Have you ever been in a situation that stretched you beyond what you were comfortable with? What was it? How did you respond?

7. Isaiah 40:31 says, "Yet those who wait for the Lord will gain new strength; they will mount up with wings like eagles, they will run and not get tired, they will walk and not become weary." Think of a time when God strength-

ened you when you were tired and weary. What were the circumstances?

8. Do you believe the saying that "opposites attract"? Why or why not?

9. Why did Parker doubt she was right for Justin? How did Meghan encourage her?

10. Meghan was attracted to Cade but afraid to let him get too close. Why? Has anything ever stopped you from allowing people to get to know the "real" you? What was it?

11. What was the turning point in Cade's faith journey?

12. Meghan was looking for a "hidden treasure" on Blue Key Island. What do you think the "real" treasure was? Why?

REQUEST YOUR FREE BOOKS!

2 FREE INSPIRATIONAL NOVELS
PLUS 2
FREE
MYSTERY GIFTS

LoveInspired®

YES! Please send me 2 FREE Love Inspired® novels and my 2 FREE mystery gifts (gifts are worth about $10). After receiving them, if I don't wish to receive any more books, I can return the shipping statement marked "cancel". If I don't cancel, I will receive 4 brand-new novels every month and be billed just $4.24 per book in the U.S. or $4.74 per book in Canada, plus 25¢ shipping and handling per book and applicable taxes, if any*. That's a savings of over 20% off the cover price! I understand that accepting the 2 free books and gifts places me under no obligation to buy anything. I can always return a shipment and cancel at any time. Even if I never buy another book, the two free books and gifts are mine to keep forever.

113 IDN ERXA 313 IDN ERWX

Name _____ (PLEASE PRINT)

Address _____ Apt. #

City _____ State/Prov. _____ Zip/Postal Code

Signature (if under 18, a parent or guardian must sign)

Order online at www.LoveInspiredBooks.com

Or mail to Steeple Hill Reader Service:

IN U.S.A.: P.O. Box 1867, Buffalo, NY 14240-1867
IN CANADA: P.O. Box 609, Fort Erie, Ontario L2A 5X3

Not valid to current subscribers of Love Inspired books.

Want to try two free books from another series?
Call 1-800-873-8635 or visit www.morefreebooks.com

* Terms and prices subject to change without notice. N.Y. residents add applicable sales tax. Canadian residents will be charged applicable provincial taxes and GST. Offer not valid in Quebec. This offer is limited to one order per household. All orders subject to approval. Credit or debit balances in a customer's account(s) may be offset by any other outstanding balance owed by or to the customer. Please allow 4 to 6 weeks for delivery. Offer available while quantities last.

Your Privacy: Steeple Hill Books is committed to protecting your privacy. Our Privacy Policy is available online at www.SteepleHill.com or upon request from the Reader Service. From time to time we make our lists of customers available to reputable third parties who may have a product or service of interest to you. If you would prefer we not share your name and address, please check here. ☐

LIREG08R

TITLES AVAILABLE NEXT MONTH

Don't miss these four stories in September

A DRY CREEK COURTSHIP by Janet Tronstad
Dry Creek
Charley Nelson wants more than friendship with Edith Hargrove.
He wants romance. But the no-nonsense widow misunderstands,
and starts lining up candidates for him to date! How can he
convince her that she's the only woman for him?

AT HIS COMMAND by Brenda Coulter
Homecoming Heroes
Everyone in Prairie Springs loves cheerful army nurse
Madeline Bright. Yet the only man to catch her eye is ex-pilot
Jake Hopkins. Jake is convinced she's better off without him,
but Maddie is determined to be part of his life. And if he's not
careful, she might conquer his heart.

A TIME TO HEAL by Linda Goodnight
Years ago, Kat Thatcher fled her hometown with a secret only
Seth Washington knew. Now she's back, and comes face-to-face
with Seth on her first day in town! He's as handsome as ever, and
available. Way too available for a woman who isn't sure she's
ready to love again.

DEEP IN THE HEART by Jane Myers Perrine
Katie Wallace left Silver Lake with big dreams…and came home
with big heartache. Silver Lake has gone on without her—so has
Rob Chambers, the boy she left behind. Can Rob forgive her and
give them both a second chance at love?